Murder on the Ridge

For Faine and Teya

KCP Fiction is an imprint of Kids Can Press

Kids Can Press acknowledges the financial support of the Government of Ontario,
through the Ontario Media Development Corporation's Ontario Book Initiative; the
Ontario Arts Council; the Canada Council for the Arts; and the Government of
Canada, through the BPIDP, for our publishing activity.

Published in Canada by   Published in the U.S. by
Kids Can Press Ltd.   Kids Can Press Ltd.
29 Birch Avenue   2250 Military Road
Toronto, ON M4V 1E2   Tonawanda, NY 14150

www.kidscanpress.com

Edited by Charis Wahl
Cover illustration and design by Céleste Gagnon

Printed and bound in Canada

CM 06 0 9 8 7 6 5 4 3 2 1
CM PA 06 0 9 8 7 6 5 4 3 2 1

Library and Archives Canada Cataloguing in Publication

Stenhouse, Ted
      Murder on the ridge / Ted Stenhouse.

ISBN-13: 978-1-55337-892-1 (bound).
ISBN-10: 1-55337-892-X (bound).
ISBN-13: 978-1-55337-893-8 (pbk.).
ISBN-10: 1-55337-893-8 (pbk.)

1. Vimy Ridge, Battle of, 1917 — Juvenile fiction.   I. Title.

PS8587.T4485M87 2006   jC813'.6   C2005-903651-6

Kids Can Press is a  Entertainment company

Murder on the Ridge

Ted Stenhouse

KCP FICTION
An Imprint of Kids Can Press

The Bloody Red Baron

I crouched behind the tall grass and bushes lining the irrigation ditch and watched the black Fargo pickup head down the lane toward me. Old Man Howe's wrinkled face peered over the steering wheel between bony, white knuckles that always seemed ready to squeeze the life out of something.

It was well past supper, and I was wondering what Old Man Howe wanted at the Samson house, when he never once stopped except to complain about me or my brother, Tim, or to bring bad news to my mom and dad.

When he swung the pickup left onto our gravel driveway, I crossed the irrigation ditch on the board bridge I'd made and headed straight across the wheat field. I stepped through the barbed wire fence on the far side and continued along Main, past the United Church to Frankie's store. It was after closing time, and the sun was getting ready to set. But I knew Frankie would open the door if I knocked hard enough. He lived in back of his store. Folks around Grayson figured he was selling vanilla extract to the Indians when the beer parlor was closed. The Blackfoot people called vanilla *saakokie*.

I was just about to pay for the jar of strawberry jam and the tin of evaporated milk I was taking to Emma Howe's shack in the woods when the black Fargo pickup crept past, the old face glaring out the side window.

Out of instinct, I ducked.

Frankie made a low chuckling sound from behind the glass-topped counter.

"What did you do?" he asked. "I hope you didn't steal from Mr. Howe?"

"I don't steal from anybody."

"You mean, not *just* anybody?"

I reached up from where I was crouched and put my money on the counter.

A second later, coins rattled above me.

I scooped up the change, grabbed the paper grocery bag and worked my way to the door.

"He's going to get you," Frankie said.

"Not if I get him first," I said and peeked out the doorway.

Frankie was still laughing when I slipped onto Main Street and crossed the gravel toward the post office. Half a block south, I crossed the train station platform and headed east along the tracks. A second later, I heard the pickup engine roar behind me. I ran hard toward the road crossing the railway tracks onto the reserve. If I got there first, I'd have a safe and easy walk for the next five miles. Old Man Howe wouldn't follow me on foot.

The black pickup skidded to a stop with the rails between the front and back tires, like the truck had a mind not to cross onto the reserve. I was hardly a yard from the door, looking back at Howe's old face staring out the side window. Before I could step back, he reached across the seat, snapped the door handle up and swung the door so quickly it threw a hot breeze across my face.

"I'll give you a ride to my daughter's house," he said. "Unless you've got a mind to walk after dark."

"I'm not scared of the dark."

He just glared like he knew I was lying.

Old Man Howe was much scarier than the dark, the one person I was really afraid of. I'd had run-ins with him before, and had even won a few of them. But I never believed they were much more than battles in a larger war I was bound to lose. My only chance of winning was if he dropped dead or if some power greater than God and Jesus and Mary and Joseph and all the angels in heaven rolled back his skin and showed the world where some little spark of decency lived.

I got in the pickup and clicked the door closed.

For a second, I imagined one of his wrinkles had turned up slightly and made the very earliest start of a smile. Then his cheeks puffed up and he let out a burp that smelled like pork chops. Before he started east toward his daughter's shack in the woods, he twisted the rearview mirror until I could see his eyes watching me.

I turned away and stared out the side window at the railway tracks crossing the slight slope that headed out onto the Blackfoot reserve. I wondered if Old Man Howe had ever been out there, if he'd ever seen Indian people living as Indians did now, or if all he'd ever thought of them was that Wilfred Black, Wolfleg to the Indian people, had married his daughter Emma. I wondered if that was all it took for him to send his daughter's husband to Vimy Ridge thirty-five years ago on that Easter Monday morning in 1917. I wondered if that was when he began hating everything Indian.

I remembered a story I'd heard while sitting on the packed dirt at the back door of the Grayson beer parlor, holding the door ajar, listening to the drinking men talk about the first war. The Christmas before the battle of Vimy Ridge, all the Canadian soldiers were huddled in their trenches waiting for the Hun to attack or waiting for orders to attack the Hun when the Red Baron's plane came sputtering over the ridge. He waggled a little wave with his wings and, in the earlier morning light, the red machine seemed to smile down at the soldiers. Then the Bloody Red Baron dived from the sky and blazed his guns not two feet from the Canadian trench. The engine sputtered again and the plane climbed, only to drop a line of green canisters tied with parachutes the size of umbrellas. While the soldiers jumped for their gas masks, the canisters hit the earth, following the pockmarked line the guns had just made. But it wasn't gas at all. It was twelve bottles of schnapps.

Howe accelerated onto the highway.

"I'm not so different from you," he said.

I turned from Vimy Ridge and cranked the window

down, letting the wind pound the inside of the pickup and swallow his words.

He didn't get mad, or cuss at me or even threaten to toss me out into the ditch. He just slowed down. Trucks and cars honked their horns as they roared past.

"I was a kid once myself," he said. "I thought I knew everything. Nobody was as smart as me. If something went wrong in the town or my family, I could make it right. I don't mean just my way. I mean right as if the good Lord had set His hand on me and willed me to do His work."

He paused as a big truck roared past, glanced at me looking at him in the rearview mirror, then grinned.

"You're a mean old man."

He laughed out loud, then broke into a coughing fit I figured might end his life right there.

"You're right on that count," he finally said. "I got smart. Now I know you're a fool, just like I was. But it's not too late. You can still change."

"Into what?" I asked, facing him directly now. "You?"

He pulled over and pushed on the brake pedal. The pickup came to a stop just as a carload of Indian people passed, the kids all pressed up against the windows, making faces and grinning at us.

"You offer me a ride, then throw me out?"

"Open the gate," was all he said.

The barbed wire gate hung loosely along the bottom edge of the ditch. It was the entrance to Emma Howe's property, the land Old Man Howe had given to Wilfred Black so he'd go to war.

I pushed open the pickup's door.

"I got something for you," Howe said.

He reached behind his left hip and pulled out a long leather wallet fastened with a chain to his waist belt. He unzipped it and removed two twenty-dollar bills. My breath nearly stopped at the sight. He folded each bill in half then in half again, reached over and slid them into my shirt pocket.

"If I'm a mean old man," he said, "let's see if you're any different."

I stared down into my pocket in disbelief.

"What's it for?" I asked. "You want me to clean out your grain bins for the rest of my life?"

Old Man Howe laughed again. "I want you to run off that Indian who's been hanging around my daughter."

"Catface?" I asked. "He's my friend. He's her grandson, your own blood."

He slapped my face and hollered, "Open the damned gate!"

I stumbled out of the pickup and fell into the ditch. When I got up and to the gate, Old Man Howe had turned the pickup around. He grinned at me from the side window.

I dropped the gate, jammed my hand into my shirt pocket, pulled out the bills and ran up the ditch bank to the gravel shoulder.

A big truck laid on its horn and nearly blew me

back into the ditch. When I got the diesel exhaust and dust rubbed from my eyes, Old Man Howe was gone, and I was left standing on the roadside with forty of his dollars in my fist.

Crazy Old Indian Stories

I stuffed the crumpled bills into my shirt pocket, re-hooked the gate and headed across the wild prairie grass toward the dark mound of woods a half mile to the south. The air around me had an odd smell, like saddle leather after a horse had been run hard. I sniffed my right hand. The stink made me jerk away. I took out the bills. At arm's length, I could still smell them. I wondered how long they'd been in Howe's wallet and how long he'd been sitting on that leather.

I pushed the bills into my back pocket and headed into the woods. I could hear Arthur and Catface talking and laughing before I could see the flickering light from the campfire. Their voices went silent, then quickly turned to whispers, followed by Arthur's loud voice.

"Friend or foe?"

For a second, I had to consider the question.

"Neither!" I said.

The whispers returned.

"Must be an ally," Arthur said before he hollered back. "Name, rank and serial number!"

"Will Samson. Dumb-head second class. And you know I can't remember numbers worth a darn."

I stepped out at the campfire, where Arthur and Catface were sitting cross-legged.

"To me." Arthur paused. "You'll always be a first-class dumb-head."

"Thanks," I said, and sat.

Arthur glanced to my left then to my right.

"Now what?"

"Weren't you supposed to bring groceries?"

"Darn," I said. "I left them in Howe's pickup."

"You caught a ride with Old Man Howe?" Arthur said. "I wondered what that smell was."

"*Kaxtomo*," Catface said, and headed into Emma's shack.

"What's wrong with him?"

"Associating with Old Man Howe makes you an enemy."

"I know *kaxtomo* means enemy, Arthur."

A few minutes later, Catface came out of the shack carrying a large brown envelope and dropped it in my lap. We'd all read the papers inside more times than I cared to remember.

"What's this for?"

"Facts," Catface said. "To remind you whose side you're on."

"I don't need any help."

"You need a bath," he said. "You even smell like him."

I leaned against the bills in my back pocket, trying

to seal the smell to the earth. I stared across the camp-fire to Arthur and Catface. Their eyes seemed to be full of fire as the flames flickered in the night air.

Catface was sixteen now, three years older than me and Arthur. He'd decided over the summer to quit school to help his grandma on their quarter section of farmland. It was late August, the harvest was coming, and he knew the work was on his shoulders. He'd grown up in Heavy Shield Residential School, so he had learned what it meant to trust people who were sup-posed to protect. Now he trusted nobody but himself.

I lowered my head until I could see the address printed on the left corner of the envelope: Govern-ment of Canada, Ottawa, Ontario. I knew what the government papers said. I'd read them a dozen times, trying to figure out some clue from the words, but it always turned out the same: Wilfred Black was killed in action on that Easter Monday morning, in the midst of a sleet storm during the Battle of Vimy Ridge. That was April 9, 1917. I thought that was the end of Wilfred Black's story.

Then a month ago — hardly a week after his mother died from thirty-five years of madness in the Ponoka Mental Asylum — a letter came for Emma. Inside, someone had placed an old letter addressed to Wilfred's mother. The paper was brown and stained with dried mud, like somebody had written it in a trench. The writing was so poor I thought somebody had used the wrong hand to write with, like he was trying to hide who he was. It was dated Easter 1917 and said "Dear Mrs. Black, Wilfred was killed by one of his own. Nobody could stop it. Everybody was too scared. He was a good soldier. He was a proud man." Then there was some very rough writing that I thought said "He talks for Indians." I figured Wilfred was saying good things about Indian soldiers while he was in the army, or maybe he was translating words so Indian soldiers and white officers could understand each other. There was no signature on the old letter. Now, thirty-five years later, the Indian people were beginning to think like Catface, that maybe Wilfred Black — Wolfleg — had been murdered on the ridge.

I leaned over and dropped the envelope next to Catface's leg. "I'm not your enemy. Not in any language. Not because I'm white, and not because I was forced to ride with Old Man Howe. No amount of money could turn me against you."

"Who said anything about money?" Arthur asked.

"Just in case you were thinking it," I said, and sat back on the dirty lump of bills in my back pocket.

"I want to find out who killed my grandpa," Catface said.

"One of his own," I said. "It was an accident, a mistake in the battle. It happens all the time. Maybe *you* should read that letter again."

"He was murdered," Arthur said. "We all know that. Old Man Howe knows it. His daughters know it. You're the only one who's confused here."

"It was thirty-five years ago. I don't know how we can find out who did it. And I sure can't see a way to prove it so it makes any difference beyond ..." My air ran down to nothing, and I took a big breath. "Besides, we're just lookin' for trouble."

Catface turned away like he'd given up on saying anything more.

"My grandpa will help us," Arthur said.

"No, he won't. He never helps except to tell crazy old Indian stories that don't make any sense to nobody but himself."

"You think Grandpa is crazy?"

"His stories are."

"They're legends," Arthur said. "Not stories. He's a medicine man. He could turn you into a gopher."

"At least a gopher wouldn't have to listen to all the crazy old talk about murder and rats in trenches and dead soldiers hanging in barbed wire."

"What would a gopher do?"

"Spend the money he found."

"Where would a gopher get money?"

"Maybe Old Man Howe gave it to him to run some Indian off his land," I said.

"What are you talking about, Will Samson? If you're trying to say something, just come out and say it."

"I'm not saying nothing. I just mean, what if that happened?"

"Like, what if Howe sent somebody to Vimy Ridge to see that Wilfred Black got killed? Or made sure somebody who was going would take care of his business?"

"I guess."

"So now you agree with us."

"Okay!" I said, and turned to Catface. "Old Man Howe gave me forty dollars to run you off his property."

Both Catface and Arthur stared at me, their eyes wide and as red as the fire.

"What are you two looking at? That's nearly two months wages for my dad."

"And you took it?" Arthur asked.

"Is that why you stink?" Catface asked.

"He tricked me. I tried to give it back but he hit me for not opening the gate. When I tried to throw it at him, I nearly got run down by a big truck hauling hogs."

Neither of them made a sound.

"Wilfred took this land," I said. "He took Howe's daughter."

"And now he's dead because of land, and Emma, and because of Old Man Howe," Catface said. "And what's wrong with his real name? Do you have a problem calling an Indian by his own name instead of the one he got in the white school?"

"It's hard to change!" I nearly shouted. "Besides, all I ever hear in town is Wilfred Black."

"This isn't town," Catface said.

"Okay, just forget I brought it up at all."

A noise came from inside the shack. The door

opened with a bang, and Emma stood wiping her dress front flat.

"Are you boys okay?" she asked. "I thought I heard arguing."

"Arthur's just scaring Will with old Indian stories." Catface laughed. "I had to poke him with a stick to make him stop screaming."

"They can be terribly scary, Will. Maybe you three ought to stick to fishing stories."

"I'm okay with Indian stories," I said.

Indian stories were even scarier than Old Man Howe, but I didn't like to admit that. The problem was they had things happening that seemed unnatural, but not pretend things, real things happening to real people. It didn't help none that Mom had made me go to church so much. I believe that made me fear anything that wasn't related to God or Jesus.

I wondered what kind of man Wolfleg had been, if he believed the white man's stories or if he was still Indian enough to believe the Blackfoot ways. I figured I could guess forever and probably never get it right. I'd have to talk to Wolfleg directly for that.

Emma said something about the groceries I had forgotten in her dad's pickup, then went inside. I figured I must have told her, but I couldn't really remember. Maybe she had seen what had happened, like she was an Indian, too, and could see beyond her place in this world.

I clamped my hands over my crossed knees and

rocked back and forth, turning my head slowly between Catface and Arthur. We sat closer and closer to the campfire as it burned down to nearly nothing, as the growing storm rumbled in the west and faint flashes of lightning blinked on and off in the distance, talking about Indian stories that made me wish it was daylight and I was chopping wood, or anything that would keep me from remembering that Indian stories are too often true, and that I'd had a couple of my own, like that night I'd spent alone on a hill that didn't exist during the day, where the wolf-like dog kept me from running from my fear; and the next night, in these very woods, when Arthur's grandpa walked into the darkness, seemed to stoop to check the earth, then continued on all fours like a wolf.

They've Sent Children to Fight

Arthur stood with his hands on his hips, looking west, the campfire's faint embers glowing red behind him. After a few seconds, he glanced over at the oiled tarp he and Catface had hung over a rope tied between two trees, making a shallow camp tent big enough for three boys who'd rather sleep outside, even in a storm.

"Oughta cut some branches and block the ends," Arthur said.

"If you don't want to get wet," I added.

As the wind whipped the tarp and strained the stakes holding the perimeter ropes to the earth, we cut down enough live branches to cover both ends of the tent. I retied the ropes with an extra knot or two. Catface leaned the live branches at either end, and Arthur wove them together. We crawled through the opening, set out our bed rolls and lay back, listening to the thunderstorm rumbling around us.

"Darn," Arthur said, "I gotta pee."

"Me too," Catface said.

"Why'd you even bring it up? Now I gotta go, too."

We crawled out under the branches and headed off in three different directions. The wind was strong now and the trees were thrashing in the night air like tall men fighting to stay standing.

Once we got back inside, hardly five minutes passed and there was nothing left to hear among the rumbles of thunder but long steady breathing.

Pretty soon, they were both snoring.

For a time, the storm seemed as if it would pass us by, leaving us to sleep in peace. I felt my breathing becoming longer and longer. After I jerked awake for the third time, I heard Arthur make a low dream-shout, something so nearly quiet it would seem like nothing but an odd breath during the day. But in the night, I knew the sound was a horrible scream from something living inside him, something he could hide from during the daylight, but had to face when he slept.

I fell asleep with the storm rolling to the east to threaten a land I had never seen. Still, I felt myself moving away from this place to the one that had haunted me since I discovered that Old Man Howe had sent Wilfred Black to die on Vimy Ridge. In my dream, I jerked upright and banged my head on the pole holding the canvas. I fought the sleep, trying to will myself awake, but I just fell further into the darkness, my head hurting from something that wasn't even real.

A loud boom jolted the air, shaking my bones loose inside my skin. Arthur stood over me in the darkness, his eyes wide and angry. "It's started. Get up." At the end of the canvas, where there had been branches, a blast of wind-driven sleet whipped past a face I knew. Wilfred Black, Catface's grandpa, glared first at me, then at Arthur. "Damn this army," he said. "They've sent children to fight." And he stomped off through the mud.

"You men," another voice called. "Anyone who's too drunk to fight, stay back or I'll put you up front. You'll get it first. There'll be no shooting our own because of a belly full of army rum." The men shouted together that they were all drunk and that they'd been ready to go up front since they got off their mother's tit. The cannon fire roared overhead. The ground rolled as if I was riding a moving train. In a flash, the night sky was as bright as daylight.

"I'm going," Arthur said, and threw me an army uniform. We dressed together and pulled on boots. They fit too big — like they were meant for men. Arthur ran out into the storm. The sleet stopped him with its force. I followed close behind and had to grab him around the shoulders or I would've knocked him over. Ahead of us, line after line of Canadian soldiers stooped under their gear as they crept up the ridge like they were in no hurry in the world. Ahead of them, not a hundred yards away, a thousand cannon shells burst in a blaze of angry red in the white sleet. Bits of barbed wire and the remains of long-dead soldiers exploded from the face of the ridge. Arthur and I ran, slipping in the muck, falling, running — trying to reach the line of men and Wilfred Black on the day he died on Vimy Ridge.

———•••——•—

Arthur screamed really loud this time, not a dreamy squeak. He lay curled in on himself, clutching his stomach like he'd been shot. Catface rolled over and adjusted his pillow under his chin.

"I told you not to eat all that jerky," he said. "Now you got the cramps."

"Just leave me alone," Arthur said.

Outside, the storm had turned back on us. Thunder clapped and shook the ground. Lightning flashed in jagged lines across the sky. Then the hail came, rattling like machine-gun fire at first, then thumping the earth like ten thousand cannons all firing on this one place.

Once in a Lifetime in Grayson

We worked all that morning cleaning up the fallen trees and branches, hardly doing any of the general fixing we'd come to do in the first place. Then, with the darn roof wrecked in the storm, we had to turn our attention to that. By late afternoon, we'd only got back to where we were when we arrived to help Emma Howe make her shack into a home.

I tried to talk to Arthur about my dream of Vimy Ridge, and later, I tried to give the forty dollars to Emma. Neither worked out.

I followed Arthur past the tarp drying in the warm August air and into a clearing a hundred yards from the cabin, where I'd seen Arthur's grandpa become something that looked more like a wolf than a man.

Arthur stood with his back to me and looked into the woods much like I had done that night, but now the bright sun lit up the woods, and all its animal shapes and twisted images that were really just living branches moved in the easy breeze, quiet and calm, like the woods were asleep. I wondered if they dreamed, and if they did, did they scream in their sleep, at horrors humans wouldn't understand?

"Do you remember when I saved you from gettin' beat up by that gang?" Arthur asked.

"Which time?"

"The first one."

"Sure," I said. "It's hard to forget gettin' your life saved by an Indian. That sort of thing doesn't happen but once in a lifetime in Grayson."

"About as uncommon as a white man savin' an Indian."

"I don't believe I've ever heard that happening," I grinned. When Arthur didn't smile, I added, "Never seen anyone throw a rock harder or truer than you did that day."

"Had to," he said. "I was so scared I figured I'd fill my pants."

"*That's* what that smell was."

Arthur shook his head. "It was the other three slipping in the stuff I scared out of them."

I laughed. "I believe it was the stuff all four of you Indians scared out of me."

Arthur half nodded and placed his hands on his hips, his elbow so close to my arm I could feel his heat. We stood there like that, not moving, letting our shirt sleeves touch in the breeze as if the woods was an old friend, just then stopping to talk.

"Where'd you see Grandpa?" Arthur asked.

I knew he meant that night nearly two months ago

when Grandpa stooped and walked on all fours.

"Over there," I said, moving my head slightly toward the twisted shadows.

"If you ask him," Arthur said, "he'll help you."

"Us," I corrected him.

"If you say so."

We stood for a while longer, letting the breeze and the woods whisper their secrets through our shirts.

"Boys!" Emma called. "Supper's on!"

Arthur started back through the woods. I watched his broad shoulders and his long, steady stride. He seemed more like a man every day. I wondered if I'd ever catch up, if Arthur would ever see me as I saw him.

The Young Are so Foolish

Emma Howe always seemed to know when I was up to something. That went all the way back to the first week of July, when I accidentally broke into her shack, and she tried to run me through with a sharpened broomstick. I never was sure if she'd planned to kill me. I was just glad she didn't. But I believe that day made her a good deal watchful around me. Now, any time Arthur and Catface and I are together, she figures there's a good chance we're up to no good. I haven't seen the broomstick since that day, but I'm afraid that it's within her reach.

She watched Catface, Arthur and me closely as we approached her door.

"You three look like you've been telling secrets."

"Mostly they were lies," I said.

"Most secrets are," Emma said. "I know what the three of you are up to."

"Cleaning up a mess," Arthur said.

In a single quick motion, she raised her hand and slapped Arthur across the ear.

"Ouch!"

"Pretty damned smart, aren't you? You know everything there's to know. Young fools," she said. "In 1914, they were signing up to fight a war like it was a game. And the ones who had the sense to stay home got handed white feathers, taunted as cowards by girls who wouldn't recognize a trench if they fell into it headfirst.

"And all the fools who missed the first war got a chance in the second. And what do the fools leave the rest of us to live with? Death and misery. All mine are dead, and for what?"

"Maybe yours didn't have to die," I said, trying to make Catface's idea of murder make some kind of sense.

I covered my ear, but she didn't even raise her hand.

"It is hard enough to live knowing that my own father sent Wilfred to war, that Wilfred's death was all that would satisfy his hateful heart," she said. "And now you say that letter from Wilfred's mother was also a lie, that Wilfred didn't die by accident either, that he was really murdered."

"But there were mud stains on the letter," I said. "And no signature anywhere. It's like somebody was sending a clue from thirty-five years ago."

After a long pause, she said, "You must be hungry."

"I am, kinda."

"That is one of the few things in this world I can fix."

Arthur rubbed his ear.

Catface shrugged as if he didn't have a clue why she'd gone on like that to Arthur. I figured Catface must have been asking too many questions about Emma's dad and the deal he made with Wilfred, giving him the land she and Catface now lived on if Wilfred would join the fighting in France.

Emma had cooked dried deer meat and onions in the bacon fat left over from breakfast. The meat looked plump and tender and smelled like pork. There were boiled beet greens and new potatoes from her garden that I had yet to find. She set it all on the table with the soda biscuits I'd smelled baking that afternoon.

We all sat at the narrow wooden table — me beside Arthur and across from Emma and Catface.

I broke off a piece of biscuit.

She slapped it out of my hand before I got it halfway to my mouth.

Catface shrugged again.

While the heat rose in my face, Emma said grace.

It took only two mouthfuls of new potatoes mashed under my fork, piled with deer meat and onions and just a bit of bacon fat, and I was in another place, one that smelled like a grandma's house should and where there was lots of good food and no reason to feel guilty about taking second helpings.

Then Catface kicked me under the table, not hard but with enough force to get my attention.

"What was that for?" I asked.

"Just trying to wake you up."

"I wasn't sleeping."

"You were pretty close," Arthur said.

I looked back at Emma.

She was fifty years old and had had a miserable life. Her own father had disowned her, had her held prisoner on this piece of land. Wilfred Black, her husband, had been killed in the first war, her son, Samuel, in the second, and she'd come as close to losing her grandson, Catface, to the war in Korea as I'd just come to getting told to leave the table for eating ahead of grace. But she survived it all. And she didn't look anything like I'd expect from those fifty years. She looked more like a mother than a grandma.

"I thought I'd have to kick you myself," Emma finally said.

"I guess I had a rough night."

Emma lifted her hand. I flinched, but the slap never came. She gently touched my face, her hand warm and soft on my cheek, the smell of the day's cooking so sweet on her skin I felt like closing my eyes.

"I don't want to hear any more talk of how Wilfred died or of getting even," she said, letting her hand fall. "The past is dead and buried. If I can let it die, surely the three of you can."

She said this to all of us, but I knew it was mostly directed at Catface, the only person who really mattered to a grandma with nothing else left.

"Wolfleg was murdered," Catface said.

Emma turned from me and Arthur as if we had disappeared from the room.

"You don't know that," she said softly. "And if you did, you can't prove it."

"That letter is all the proof I need."

"What good does all this suspicion serve?" she asked. "Wilfred is still buried in Flanders. Samuel is at the bottom of the sea. And there are things that I have done that I don't want to remember either."

Her eyes clouded over, and she had to stop awhile to get her breath back.

"But you are with me," she said, moving her hand down Catface's forearm until she gripped his hand. "The young are so foolish. White crosses and memories."

Catface turned from her gaze but not her touch, moving his eyes to the pictures I had first seen when I broke in, the old picture of Emma at sixteen, a baby in her arms, and Wilfred Black, Wolfleg, standing at her side, wearing his new uniform. Other than the hole in the roof from the storm and the bright light of the afternoon sun, the room looked the same as it had two months ago.

"You could forgive them," she finally said.

"Which ones?" Catface asked.

"All of them. Even me."

It's More than Indians and Whites

Catface finished eating, pushed his plate to the center of the table and tipped his head toward the door. The next minute, Arthur and I were stacking broken poplar limbs, and Catface was trimming off the small branches with a hatchet, turning the limbs into new roof timbers. Inside, Emma was rattling plates and cups in the galvanized washing tub.

Catface drove the hatchet blade deep into a standing tree. "I don't care what she says."

"It was a long time ago," Arthur said. "Maybe you should let it be."

"I still want to know."

"Think about all the things that have happened to us." Arthur wasn't talking to either me or Catface, or didn't seem to need an answer if he was. "Yellowfly getting nearly killed by the gang of Indian haters in Grayson. Catface finding out he's got a white grandma. That Old Man Howe is his blood relation. That he owns a piece of Howe's land. That Howe had Catface's father and grandpa sent to war, hoping they'd die."

He stared at Catface for a few long seconds before he turned to me and made a motion like he expected me to answer.

"I don't know, Arthur. I guess I never thought about it all together like that."

"I used to think it was Indians against whites," he said. "Now I don't know."

"Come on, Arthur," Catface said. "That's all it's ever been. That's all it will ever be."

Arthur slowly shook his head as he thought.

"It's more than Indians and whites. It's Old Man Howe and Indians, and it's Old Man Howe and poor whites," he said, not looking at me. "Howe and the people who think like him. The Mounties. And people we haven't even thought of."

"What people?" I asked.

"I don't know. Just people. Anybody."

"What if we find out things we don't want to know?" I asked. "Emma doesn't want to know everything either."

Catface gave me a look that meant I should watch my mouth. "I want to know who killed Wolfleg."

"I'm sick of fighting over this," I said. "I don't care what we find out. I just want to get it over with."

We went back to stripping branches, not saying what was to be done. It didn't matter to me. I had decided to figure it out, no matter what I found, no matter how bad it turned out to be. Besides, it was what I was good at — digging a big hole for myself, filling it with more trouble than a soul could sort out in two lifetimes, then jumping in headfirst.

General de Gaulle of France

We got up early on Sunday morning. After breakfast, I said I'd get some tar paper to waterproof the roof in a day or two, that the roof should be good for one rain, if it wasn't a heavy storm. Emma told me to make sure to tell my dad that she would pay him for any material we used and that if I wasn't back in time to finish her roof, she'd come looking for me, maybe with a sharpened broomstick. I tried to smile, but even though I knew she was joking, I couldn't do it.

It was hardly eight o'clock when Arthur and I left Emma's shack, but the sun was bright and hot and the air felt like mid-afternoon. All through breakfast, I'd been thinking about the forty dollars I'd got from her dad, how maybe I'd hide it somewhere for her to find. But I knew that wouldn't work, especially after she'd waved the bills away like they were carrying a horrible disease.

Arthur kept glancing over at me as we walked down the railway tracks, heading west toward Grayson. He looked like he was working up to asking me something awfully important, but never did. Unless the same old question was something worth asking.

"So what's your plan?"

"I could sure go for a Coke at Gunther's gas station."

Arthur gave me a look. "You ask stupid questions too."

"I know," I said, "but they're not usually the same one."

"But it's the same old stupid answer."

I didn't have anything worth saying, but said something anyway.

"We could write a letter to General de Gaulle of France and ask him if he saw anything suspicious on Vimy Ridge," I said. "He was probably somewhere nearby. After all, Vimy Ridge is in France, and I don't believe France is anywhere near as big as Canada."

"Sure," Arthur said, "or we could swim across the Atlantic this afternoon and have a talk with him."

"Don't be stupid. It'd take us all afternoon just to get to the ocean at Halifax."

"We could swim overnight." Arthur draped his arm over my shoulder. "Unless you're still scared of the dark."

"I got over that two nights ago," I said, still thinking of my dream, and set my arm on his opposite shoulder.

"How long do you figure it'd take to find out anything worth repeatin' from this Frenchman?"

"Well, we'd have to learn the language first."

"We could have breakfast while we're learnin'."

"Get our asking done by noon," I said. "Then swim to Halifax and walk west down the tracks 'til we hit

Grayson. Should be back by suppertime."

"I don't think so," Arthur said.

"Why not?"

"It's a different time in France."

"Darn, I forgot about that," I said. "I guess that plan's ruined."

"Got any others?"

"We could walk to Vancouver and swim the Pacific."

"We'd gain a couple hours at least." Arthur grinned.

"We could be home before we left."

We both stopped as if we had the same thought. We turned, then slowly looked back down the tracks.

"Well, I'll be darned," Arthur said. "There we come now."

"And just look at us," I said. "We got everything figured out. Maybe we should save ourselves some swimming and just go ask us."

"Nah," Arthur said. "That's got to be a mile of extra walking."

We turned back and headed on down the tracks.

We got to the irrigation ditch and the big wooden culvert by about ten o'clock. The cool water churned at the culvert's mouth, then disappeared under the tracks. We undressed like it was a race, leaving only our underwear to cover ourselves. Arthur jumped in head-first and was swept under the railway tracks. A second later, I was in the water, the faint image of Arthur's feet kicking in the bubbles ahead of me, becoming black for a second under the rails, then bright with white foam bursting all around as he broke the surface.

I popped out beside Arthur, my hair stuck to my forehead, our feet and arms touching every now and then as we treaded water. When he glanced at the jagged scar running down my left breast — the one that looked like I'd earned the right to be called a warrior — I pushed his head under and swam to shore. I got out of the water a few steps ahead of him, walked back over the mound of rocks that held the ties and rails and down the other slope and dressed.

"Hey," Arthur said, following me, "I hardly think about that anymore. It's your scar. You got it in battle."

"It wasn't much of a battle," I said. "It was more of an accident."

"I just wish I had one of my own. Then Grandpa would tell me stuff like he tells you."

"I don't understand your grandpa."

"He's an old Indian with old ideas."

We walked back up the slope and stood, me facing the dirt trail heading north to my house, Arthur looking west toward his house.

"I better get home before Dad finds out I've been hanging around with an Indian."

"Yeah," Arthur said, "I'll probably lose my scalp when my dad smells white man on me."

We headed off in our different directions, but whenever I glanced back over my shoulder to look at Arthur, he was just turning to look at me.

I Felt Guilty

As I walked home, I wished I could give my scar to Arthur. I knew the scar would mean more to him than it means to me. It's important to me, too, just not as important as it would be to an Indian, especially considering it looked like I got it at a Sundance ceremony, where young Indians dance against the medicine pole until they tear sticks from their flesh, becoming not just men but also warriors. And I got it only because I'd surprised Emma when I barged into her shack, a stranger to her, and she was so scared she stuck me with a sharpened broomstick she kept under her bed for protection.

I felt guilty that I'd been marked as if I was brave and that Arthur hadn't been, especially when he was the brave one. And now Arthur's grandpa looked at me differently because of a scar I'd got only because I'd been a fool. He kept saying it meant more than any white man would ever know, but I didn't believe him. I wished it was Arthur who'd been scarred, and I wished he'd get mad at me like he used to when he saw it. At least then, I'd know why I always felt guilty.

Ever since Arthur rescued me from the gang of Indian kids trying to beat me senseless when we were both six, I've felt guilty about one thing or another. First, I didn't know why an Indian would help a white kid, then I worried that maybe I wouldn't help Arthur if things got really tough, that one day I'd wake up and I'd've turned into a white man who lived in town, and that Arthur would be just another Indian on the reserve.

He'd Rather Be Fishing

When I got home, Tim was sitting on the front steps in his best white shirt and a shiny black bow tie. In a second, I remembered. It was Sunday morning. Before I could run, Tim called, "Hi, Will ... Mom, Will's back! We can all go to church now!"

I gave him a dirty look.

Tim shrugged like he could do nothing to help me now.

Mom said some pretty loud, rough-sounding words inside the house. Even though I felt guilty for being late, I could tell the words weren't meant for me. Somebody else was in trouble for a change.

"I don't give a tinker's darn what you think, woman!" Dad said. "You're not making me wear a hunk of cloth around my neck!"

"It's a tie," Mom said.

"Well, go tie up something with it."

Then there was a pause where all I heard were low voices, a chair sliding on the floor and finally a loud bump.

"Get your hands off my neck!" Dad said.

"Hold still!" Mom said.

A good deal of grumbling was followed by a long silence. Tim and I turned our heads as if trying to hear whispers. Then, in a single quick move, Tim stood, grabbed my arm and pulled me back from the steps.

The door flew open and Dad came stomping out across the porch and down the stairs.

"What are you two staring at?" Dad asked, with the long black tie hanging off to one side of his white shirt, like it was trying to hide under his arm. "If I get one smirk, there'll be a tanning for somebody."

Tim did his best not to laugh out loud. Instead, he snorted. That sent both of us into a fit of breathless giggles so bad I figured even Dad's worst tanning wouldn't have brought us out of it.

"Jesus, Mary and Joseph," Dad said, then stomped off to the pickup, jerked the door open and sat behind the steering wheel. "Hurry up in there! If I'm not waitin' for kids, I'm waitin' for a woman."

"Will!" Mom called, "it's your turn."

Now Dad was laughing at me.

Mom just pointed to the bedroom where Tim and I slept.

I changed into the clothes Mom had set out for me in case I got home in time for church and combed my hair flat. She glanced at my bow tie and smiled, then she put her arm in the bend of my elbow, and we walked outside to the pickup.

"Well, I'll be darned," Dad said.

I held the passenger door open. Dad had covered the seat of our old pickup with a clean blanket. Mom gave me a polite smile and got in, resting her purse on her lap as she took a long, peaceful breath.

I climbed into the truck box and sat with Tim on the straw bale pushed up against the cab.

"Nice bow tie." Tim grinned.

"Why don't you shut up?"

Our pickup rumbled and jiggled and jerked and Dad pumped the clutch and cussed in a polite manner as he ground gears every time he shifted.

I thought about church and all the things I'd learned while trying to get out of going, all the words the reverend had said, and all the ways my mind fit those words into my everyday life. When I started day-dreaming about Jesus coming into our church and sitting down beside me wearing His own black bow tie and saying He'd rather be fishing, I knew I was in trouble, even though I agreed with Him on most things.

They're the Same Guy

Mom said we were to sit together like other families did because this was a special day: Dad had come to church and it wasn't even his funeral. I was made to sit next to Tim, who was next to Mom, who was next to Dad, who was sweating like he was closer to the Other Place, where redemption was most needed. We were near the back because we were late compared to people who really wanted to go to church and didn't have to be dragged.

Mom tried not to smile too much as she caught a town lady turn and notice us all together. Having her whole family in church was probably Mom's main goal in life. If she was struck down, right then, for any reason, she'd go a happy mom.

Dad's face was red from heat and lack of air. Before Mom could get her clean white hankie from her purse, he had lifted his tie and mopped at the sweat beading on his forehead.

The reverend came in and stared at us all — me in particular — like he was deciding who he should make an example of, who he would recommend for the Big Trip into the Basement, as he called the fiery place out of politeness. And this was the United Church, which was easier than anything I'd heard about the Catholic Church, where I believe a fellow like me started in the basement and had to work seventy or eighty years just to get up to the main floor, never mind even being considered for upstairs. At least as a United, I was only mostly a sinner and got to start on the main floor, on more or less equal footing with everyone else.

The reverend moved his eyes down the row of Samsons, paused at Mom with something that could pass for a smile, moved across Dad and started preaching.

We got up and prayed. We sat down. We got up and sang to Jesus. We sat down. He told us a story that meant we were all sinners. We got up and prayed. We sat down. He told us we had to give our hearts to Jesus. We got up and sang a song.

I was rubbing my rear end from all the getting up and sitting down when Arthur came walking up the aisle. He had his head down like he was afraid that if he looked up and somebody saw he was an Indian he'd get thrown out of the church and maybe even laughed at.

He inched in beside me and sat.

Mom got a glance from the town ladies. This time they didn't smile.

When we all stood to sing, Arthur turned his head a little in my direction.

"When I come to this pla–ace," Arthur sang, "I feel the Great Spir–rit."

"You talk like tha–at," I sang back, "my God will send you to the base–ement."

"No he wo–on't."

"Why no–ot?"

"Because they're the sa–ame guy."

Mom elbowed Tim. Tim elbowed me. And I would've elbowed Arthur, but he started singing the song at the top of his lungs, just the way it was written in the hymn book.

When we sat down again, Arthur leaned so close to me, I could feel his lips brushing up against the tiny hairs on my ear.

"Grandpa wants to help us with Wolfleg," he whispered. "He wants you to come to a sweat lodge."

"What's a sweat lodge?" I whispered back.

"An Indian church," Arthur said. "Except the Great Spirit really comes."

"Sure He does."

"You'll see," Arthur said, just before we got up to pray again.

We bowed our heads. Mumbled. Then sat down.

An elbow worked its way down from Mom. This time Arthur got it.

He's One of Ours

Arthur headed for the door with the last "Amen," trying to get out before the reverend could get there and check the eyes of his congregation as he shook each hand, making sure the devil had been pushed from his sight.

But Widow Bowman, all six feet and two hundred pounds of her, got to her usual spot ahead of Arthur and blocked the door.

Arthur tried to reach around her, but she slapped his hand down.

A second later, the reverend was shaking the same hand.

"Welcome to our church, young man," he said in his after-church voice.

"I'm not just a young man. I'm Arthur." Arthur tried to pull away, but the reverend wouldn't release his grip.

"The words you were singing," the reverend said, "they were different from the rest of the congregation."

"I can't remember the words to songs too good."

"No, I suppose not."

"I'll work on it for next time."

"I have a feeling you won't be coming back," the reverend said softly. "Not if you place your heathen god on the same level as the true Lord."

"The Great Spirit?" Arthur said in a loud voice, shaking his hand loose from the reverend's.

Widow Bowman looked like she might take a swing at Arthur, but he ducked around her.

I passed behind Mom as the reverend shook her hand and said he was pleased to see the Samson family all at one sitting.

When I got to Arthur, he was wiping his hand on his pant leg.

"Come on," Arthur said. "Let's get outta here."

I glanced up at Mom.

She was still shaking the reverend's hand, but she was looking at me and Arthur. Next to her was Tim. Behind them, I could see Dad looking like he was trying to sneak around the rest of the family like I had just done.

Mom mouthed "Go" to us.

"Can I stay overnight?" I called back.

She nodded quickly, then shooed us with her free hand.

Dad was behind her now, trying to make himself smaller than he really was, trying to escape unseen. The reverend caught him at the last second. As Mom walked down the stairs toward me and Arthur, I heard the reverend say, "I haven't seen you before. But I believe I can surmise your name is Samson."

"That's right," Dad said.

"Is that your whole family then?"

"That's the lot."

"And the Indian?"

"He's one of ours," Dad said. "Or might as well be."

Mom stepped quickly along the concrete sidewalk leading to the road and the line of cars and trucks waiting for all the churchgoers.

"Go now," Mom said to me and Arthur.

We were across the road that led north to the main highway and headed down Main Street twenty yards when we heard Dad's voice.

"Darn, Mom," Dad said. "That's why I don't like coming to this place. A fella has to do things just so or you're not worth nothin'."

"Shush," Mom said.

"You better be home by dinner tomorrow," Dad called after me.

"Dad —" Mom shushed him again.

"Well, he's leavin' me with all his work."

"I'll get my work caught up!" I called back, then headed down Main Street.

"Darn right you will."

"Jim Samson," Mom said, "this is church time."

I didn't turn to see what Mom was doing, but I'd bet she was glancing around, maybe even shrugging at any of the town ladies who were whispering about Dad. I didn't believe Dad was purposefully trying to get out of any future trips to church, but I did believe he just had.

Grandpa Was at
Vimy Ridge

I watched the back of Arthur's neck as we walked away from the church. Though his skin was deep brown from him being outside most of the summer, I could still see a touch of red along the line of his shirt collar, like I'd seen early in the summer. But it wasn't the sun making Arthur's neck red this time. It was anger.

Most things about the white man bothered Arthur. I accepted that in him. Some I understood and agreed with. Like how the Indians lost their land with just a piece of paper covered in lies. But I never really understood how the Great Spirit could have been on this land or in the water or in the air for more time than even Jesus. I didn't know much about being a United or about church or even Sunday school, but I couldn't believe the Indian god had much over the white one, especially Jesus.

Once we crossed the railway tracks and headed up the line toward his house, Arthur breathed easier, like the closeness of the reserve calmed his spirit.

"I thought your grandpa was camping at Horse Shoe Backwater," I said.

"He is."

"So how'd you get to talk to him? Did he come to your dream and give you a message?"

"No," Arthur said, "he used the telephone."

"You've got a telephone?"

"No."

"Oh, I see. He telephoned in your dream."

"He called Heavy Shield School and left a message for my dad."

"Wow," I said. "There's a telephone at Horse Shoe Backwater? Last time I was there, all I saw was trees and water and a couple'a tepees."

"Jeez, Will. He walked to the ferry crossing and used old Tommy Mills' telephone."

"Tommy Mills has a telephone?"

Arthur gave me the elbow I'd been expecting since church.

"So?" I said, after I was done rubbing my ribs.

"So what?"

"What's Grandpa's message? Is he still getting all sweaty in that lodge thing he does while he talks to the Indian spirits?"

"He said to get your white hide to Horse Shoe Backwater. And get ready to talk to some crazy, dead Indians."

"I could do that," I said. "It sounds like fun. Besides, I haven't talked to a crazy Indian for about a minute now."

"Okay, so that isn't exactly what Grandpa said. But

he did say 'Don't bother bringing extra clothes because you're going to be naked most of the time.'"

I turned and started back the way we had come.

Arthur caught my baggy shirttail and pulled until I stopped.

"Only in the sweat lodge," he said. "And it's as black as a coal mine at night in there."

"Nobody'll see anything?"

"Not one little thing."

"Okay, but I don't plan to walk all that way."

"Dad's got Watcher's team and wagon."

"Watcher? I thought he disappeared after he helped us catch the gang of Indian haters for beating Yellowfly."

"Well, he's back. And the last time I looked, he had straw bales on his wagon. We'll sleep the whole way to Horse Shoe Backwater."

"I don't know," I said. "I don't like the idea of dreaming about crazy, old Indian spirits."

"Can't be worse than the screaming dream you had at Emma's."

"I thought you were asleep."

"The stomach cramps got me up."

"Okay, maybe I screamed once," I said. "Dreaming about Vimy Ridge is about as bad as dreams get."

Arthur warned me that there were things I'd have to know about a sweat lodge before I went inside, not just that everybody was naked. There was a special place for all of Grandpa's pouches of sacred plants and his pipe at the head of the pit that held the heated river rocks — they had to be set out in a special way, and I might be asked to do this as a way of showing respect to Grandpa and the Indian spirits.

I didn't want to look like a fool, so I listened.

Then Arthur said that the sweat lodge was not a place white men got to go unless they were invited.

"I know," I said. "Kind'a like going to church."

"I don't think so."

"I heard that some people talk in a funny language. Sometimes their eyes go all crazy. They might even fall down and wiggle around on the floor."

"I wasn't talking about gettin' drunk."

"That's not funny, Arthur."

"I know," he said, and put his arm across my shoulder. "Grandpa likes it when you call him Grandpa, like it's his name."

I didn't answer with anything but an easy nod. I knew his grandpa liked that, like maybe I was related to him. He'd been that way ever since I got the wound on my chest. I didn't like to think about all the things being brave might mean to that man. By my age he'd been a warrior and had ridden with Lame Bull, Red Crow and Crowfoot. The thought raised a shiver all up my spine.

Arthur squeezed my shoulder as if he was waking me from a dream. He went on to say that I had to be very careful when Grandpa opened his pouches of sacred plants. He said Grandpa would pinch some and throw it on the hot rocks, but I should be careful not to breathe the smoke too deeply. And when his pipe came to me, I should only pretend to smoke, that my mind would not understand the language he spoke but my heart would, and that I should be careful when asked if I want a prayer said for me, that I might get what I asked for, and nobody would be to blame for that but me.

When we got to the gravel road in front of Arthur's house, he stopped and stared straight ahead.

"Grandpa was at Vimy Ridge," he said, like he'd finally got up enough nerve to say what was in the message from Horse Shoe Backwater.

"Your grandpa? Why didn't you tell me before all this started?"

"I didn't know."

"How couldn't you know? He's your grandpa —" I stopped. Something didn't seem right. "That's not possible. Grandpa'd be too old. Even thirty-five years ago, he'd be too old to go to war. Nobody's army would take him."

"I didn't say it was thirty-five years ago."

"Don't start any crazy, old Indian stuff."

Arthur didn't listen. "He was there last night. And many other nights."

Those words made the hairs on the back of my neck stand up. In a second, my skin felt damp and cold like I'd just been standing over my own grave. Then I thought that maybe I could just ask Grandpa what he saw, if he knew who killed Wilfred Black. But that passed quicker than it came as I remembered how Grandpa never made it easy for me, how he made me do things as if I was brave.

Now my dream of Vimy Ridge rushed back into my head, with all the pictures I'd seen of the Great War: dead bloated horses, craters big enough to hold a company of men, the rim oozing with poison gas, rats clawing and gasping, and me lying facedown in the mud and the sleet, among the chalk-white bones of those long dead.

It's Good to See
Them Again

Arthur's dad had tossed the straw bales off Watcher's wagon to make room for the tepee poles and the buffalo robes that would cover them. The rest of the space was used up by things for Arthur's mom: food, blankets and a folding chair. When I tried to set up the chair to sit on, she said if I wanted comfort I should have brought my own.

So I sat in my usual place, beside Arthur at the back of the wagon with my feet hanging over the edge of the wooden deck.

After five hours of bumping and rocking along prairie trails, my rear end felt like I'd been sitting on a sanding machine, and the rest of my body was numb, from my toenails up to my cowlick.

I pushed off the wagon and rubbed my rear end. Arthur's dad turned the horses and wagon along a wagon trail cutting through dense underbrush and on into a green meadow.

In the middle of the meadow was Grandpa's tepee. A row of painted buffalo formed an unbroken line around the hides. The door, a square flap of buffalo hide, was open. Inside were piles of blankets.

I expected to see a line of smoke coming from the V-shaped opening at the top. Arthur's grandpa usually had smoke coming from something related to his Indian medicine. But not today.

I stretched as I walked to the steep bank bordering the backwater. At the bottom, Arthur's grandpa sat on the edge of an old beaver lodge that time had worn down to a shallow mound of sticks and mud as hard as blacktop.

The water was pale green, clear and deep.

Arthur's grandpa put his finger to his lips and pointed to the opposite shore. There, a cow buffalo and her calf were knee-deep in the water. The calf was drinking. The cow had her head up, water dripping from her mouth as she watched us.

I sat cross-legged beside Arthur's grandpa. His thick gray hair hung loose down both sides of his face.

He was as big as any man I'd ever seen. His palms were as wide as two-by-six planks and as hard as buffalo hooves. His shoulders made even the biggest shirt sold in Grayson look like it was for a child. I'd figured he was at least a hundred years old. He had ridden with Lame Bull in Montana before Crowfoot and Macleod signed Treaty Number 7 in 1877, and other Indians respected him for the old ways and the medicine he performed. But after I saw him beat two armed and determined men in the woods surrounding

Emma Howe's shack, then walk through the darkness in the shape of a wolf, I wondered if maybe he wasn't much older than just a hundred human years, if maybe he wasn't something wild and primitive.

"*Istaykaytau*, buffalo cow with suckling," he said, translating for me. "They came some time in the dark last night. It's good to see them again."

"Arthur said you sent a message for me."

Grandpa stared across the backwater at the buffalo. "*Kixkixt*," he said.

"I don't understand."

"Now and then," he said. "You worry too much about time."

"Dad always says I need to get a move on."

"I agree."

"But you said —"

"Go help at camp. There's a tepee to put up." He grinned. "Get a move on."

His eyes were nearly black, with fine yellow lines running out from the pupils. They were as clear and deep as the backwater.

When I stood, the cow buffalo shifted her heavy body and moved from the water up the opposite bank and disappeared into the brush and trees lining the far shore.

Her calf tried to climb the bank too quickly and fell on its chest in the soft clay. It let out a bawl, got to its feet and ran after its mother.

"Arthur said you were on Vimy Ridge."

Grandpa just pointed to a cloud of dust rising a quarter mile from the far shore. The shape of a large dark buffalo stood in the cloud.

"Papaistamik."

He didn't have to tell me what that Blackfoot word meant. I'd heard it before. *Papaistamik* — buffalo bull in a dream. But this one was real. I knew Indian people believed dreams were as real as anything in life, but thinking like that always made me nervous. Sometimes, I was afraid to sleep.

He picked up his fishing rod and flipped the lure to the edge of the weed bed, the brown flower tops, long past their season, floating on the surface.

"How come you never talk to me except when you want me to listen?" I asked. "How come you never answer my questions?"

He turned his head slowly, past the dust settling over the buffalo bull, to the band of black clouds rising in the west.

"There's a storm coming," he said, and turned back to his fishing.

"Will!" Arthur called. "Where are you?"

"Down here!" I called back, and headed up the slope.

Behind me, Grandpa had reeled up the lure and flipped it out to the edge of the weed bed.

"Vimy Ridge," I heard him whisper. *"Kixkixt.* Now and then."

There's Trouble Coming

When I got to the top of the bank, Arthur was look-ing out over the backwater.

"Did you see the buffalo?" I asked.

"What buffalo?"

"The cow and the calf," I said. "Grandpa said they came in the night. He said it was good to see them again."

"Is that what you were talking to?"

"Of course not, Arthur. You don't think I'd talk to a buffalo?"

I turned with my hand out like I was showing him something that was pretty clear to anybody who wasn't blind. But Grandpa wasn't sitting on the beaver dam. He wasn't anywhere. His fishing rod was gone. There was no sign of the cow and the calf or the bull. I was glad I hadn't mentioned I'd seen *Papaistamik*, buffalo bull in a dream.

"But I saw Grandpa," I said.

Arthur nodded and grinned. Then he pointed east half a mile to an elbow in the backwater. There, set back from the steep bank, stood a small dome made from bent branches covered with buffalo robes. It was Grandpa's sweat lodge. Not far away were the remains of a large fire, burned down to a mound of smoldering red embers. Bits of white ash hovered in the heat waves rising from the dead fire. The shape of *Papaistamik* formed in the memory of the sweat lodge fire and moved slowly with the breeze up the trail, disappearing across the prairie.

"Grandpa's doing a sweat," Arthur said. "He's been in there most of the afternoon."

"How do you know?"

"Watcher told me," Arthur said. "He's at the camp. He said he's not going to set up a tepee for someone else to sleep in." Arthur pulled my shirt sleeve. "Come on, Dad needs help."

"I know what I saw."

"Grandpa just wants you warmed up for the sweat tonight."

"Warmed up?"

"Yeah," Arthur said. "So he doesn't scare you all the way back to England."

"England?"

"Sure. Isn't that where you Samsons are from? Isn't Samson an English name?"

"No," I said, "it's a Manitoba name."

"Well then, he doesn't want to scare you back to Manitoba."

"He's not going to scare me anywhere I don't want to go."

A second later, Arthur's mom came walking up the dip in the wagon trail that led out of the clearing. I wondered then if this was the place where the Indian god had placed his own tepee, way back when the Blackfoot people were just dreams in the smoke of his sweat lodge.

"If you two don't help set up camp," she said, "I'm going to sit on my folding chair and watch you do all the cooking and cleaning."

That's all it took and we were both running across the thick brown prairie grass and on into the shade with its lines of yellow sunlight cutting through the tall poplars.

At the clearing, not much had happened. Arthur's dad and Watcher sat in a piece of shade, their backs resting against the back tire of the wagon. They were both smoking hand-rolled cigarettes and looking very relaxed. They'd unhitched the horses, but had done little else.

Arthur and I dragged everything off the wagon, set poles and robes and ropes and blankets and food and everything in piles, sorted them, then started setting up.

"Not there," Arthur's dad said. "The smoke will blow into Grandpa's tepee. He makes enough smoke without help from you two."

We moved it and started over.

"What way does the wind blow?" Arthur's dad asked.

Arthur and I pointed west.

"Well?"

We pulled the mass of buffalo hides off and turned them a half circle around the tepee poles.

"I feel pretty stupid," I said to Arthur.

"You are."

"You're not so smart yourself," I said. "You're an Indian. You oughta know how to set up a tepee."

Arthur elbowed me.

I elbowed him back.

He let out a whoop and was on me. I tumbled backward and tried to roll him off, but he got me in a headlock. I set my teeth on his forearm and bit down hard enough to let him know I might take a chunk of flesh. Arthur released his grip. That was a mistake. I rolled hard to the right and broke loose. When he went to chase me, I sprung on him and wrapped my arm tightly around his neck and locked my wrist with the other hand.

"Now who feels stupid?" I grunted.

"I'll get Grandpa to turn you into a gopher."

I pulled hard on my arm. "All he does is make people see things that aren't really there."

"Wait 'til you're covered in brown fur and you've grown a tail that won't stop flicking," Arthur said, just before he bent my little finger back so far I thought he'd break it off.

"Ouch!"

"Where's my chair?" Arthur's mom called. "I need to sit and watch somebody else cook for a change."

In under a second, Arthur and I were back to setting up camp. I kept expecting to get jumped when my back was turned. The sneak attack was a favorite of Arthur's, but it never happened. I guess he was more afraid of getting stuck doing girls' work than getting even with me. I figured I could use that to my advantage, but gave up on the idea when Arthur's mom motioned for me to help her make the bannock. She was nearly white with flour because a gust had whipped through the camp and covered her with her work. I felt sorry for her, but not sorry enough to help.

Just as we were finishing, Arthur's grandpa came through the woods on an overgrown path leading from the sweat lodge. He had a big grin on his face and seemed full of beans.

"I saw a cow buffalo with a calf," he said. "It was good to see them again."

I glanced at Arthur, but he was acting like he was more interested in what was coming next than that I'd been right about the buffalo.

"Where?" Arthur's dad asked.

"In a vision."

I felt Arthur turn to me, but I was looking the other way.

Both Arthur's dad and Watcher walked to meet Grandpa. They stood together for a long time, talking in low Blackfoot words. Grandpa spoke a word I'd heard before.

"*Kixkixt.*"

Now and then, I thought. The word he had used about Vimy Ridge.

All three men turned and stared at me.

"Whispering men," Arthur's mom said. "There's trouble coming."

Arthur moved back and forth between the piles of blankets and the tepee as he arranged the inside for sleeping. I listened to the words the men spoke.

Over the past months, especially since I got my scar, Grandpa had been speaking to me in Blackfoot as if I understand it. Some words he translated for me when I looked too confused to ever figure them out. I had picked up some words on my own, but they were mostly cuss words. Even in Blackfoot, it's not hard to tell when somebody's cussing. I'd gotten a few of those words from Indian men on the streets of Grayson when they figured I'd done something pretty stupid. But Grandpa and Watcher and Arthur's dad spoke old-sounding, mysterious words that left me with a feeling, like Arthur's mom had said, that "there's trouble coming."

Our Mistakes Don't Guide the Spirits

I didn't want to go into the sweat lodge. I was afraid I'd do all the things Arthur told me not to do.

Don't breathe the smoke from Grandpa's sacred plants.

Don't smoke his pipe.

Don't ask for a prayer if you don't really want that thing to come into your life.

I repeated the words over and over in my mind, but all the don'ts slipped away, like the Indian spirits were ordering me to do something I didn't want to do.

Breathe the smoke.

Smoke the pipe.

Ask for a prayer.

Finally, all that was left were the words "breathe," "smoke" and "prayer."

Still, I followed Arthur down the narrow path to the elbow in the backwater, where Grandpa's fire blazed again as it heated the round river rocks.

It seemed to take hardly any time at all and Arthur's dad and Watcher were working the blackened shovels in the red embers, rolling only the unbroken rocks onto the shovels' blades and carrying them to the pit at the center of the sweat lodge.

Behind us, the band of thunderheads had grown into a deep black arch, churning and boiling.

It was nearly dark when Grandpa looked down at me from the far side of the fire.

"Take my pipe and my bundles," he said, holding them out. "Go around the lodge three times and put them in my place."

I held the Indian magic in front of me, resting them in my upturned hands, walking slowly, like I was a small child carrying an overfull drinking glass. When I got to the sweat lodge, I stared at the opening. The dome was as high as my waist, and the opening would be tight to crawl through. My neck got hot. My arms ached. Was I supposed to go inside and crawl around the fire pit three times, or was I supposed to walk around the outside? I should have listened better.

Now I was in trouble.

I stooped to go inside.

Arthur hollered from the fire, "The outside!" He made a circular motion with his finger.

I walked quickly around the outside of the sweat lodge three times, then stooped through the opening and set Grandpa's pipe and sacred bundles at the front of the rock pit, nearest the entrance.

When I backed out to face the Indian men, I knew I'd done it all wrong. Arthur's grandpa wouldn't sit at the entrance. That didn't make sense. I'd wrecked all their plans. I felt like a fool, like the last person an Indian spirit would pick to be an Indian.

Watcher put his hand on my shoulder as we stood looking at the dying fire.

"I got it wrong the first time, too," he said. "I'll move them to their right place. Nobody'll know."

"Will the sweat lodge still work?"

"Our mistakes don't guide the spirits," he said. "If they did, the spirits would have no time for anything else."

I breathed a sigh of relief. Almost right away, I was sure the sigh was also a wrong thing to do.

You Are a Brave

Arthur held the buffalo robe back from the sweat lodge opening. Watcher bent over and looked inside. I could tell he was moving Grandpa's pipe and bundles to their rightful place.

I stood beside Grandpa near the fire, not wanting to go inside the lodge, not wanting to find out things the way he found out things, not wanting to be tormented by things that weren't even real.

All around us, the thunder had grown into a steady, low rumble, like distant guns.

He touched my shoulder. His big hand felt heavy, as if it would push me into the earth.

"Minapitsixtat."

I tried to remember the word but couldn't. When I turned to him, he just smiled and nodded.

"Do not worry yourself."

"But I don't want to see Wilfred Black, I mean Wolfleg, get killed."

"You don't have to do the sweat."

"I can stay out here?" I asked, then went quiet as Arthur's dad and Watcher returned from the sweat lodge and checked the fire for any rocks they'd missed.

I waited for them to leave before I spoke again.

"You won't think I'm a coward?" I asked. "You won't think the scar was just an accident?"

"Matsi."

"I don't understand."

"Brave."

"I don't feel brave."

"You are a *matsi.*"

I moved to Arthur's side, took the buffalo robe from his hand and held it back against the dome of the sweat lodge. The rumble grew and the lightning flickered in the darkness, spreading over the land with a fury I was afraid was meant for me.

Poison Gas

The sky was dark and moonless as I undressed, folded my clothes and stacked them neatly at the base of a poplar tree thirty feet from the sweat lodge. Though no one could see anything worth talking about, I covered myself with my hands, as if that was the way I always stood.

Grandpa set a pair of rubber boots next to the lodge entrance and grinned as he put a sock in each.

"These are for my white guest," he said, and smiled as he glanced at the thunderheads. "As long as they're not full of water when the spirits are done with him."

His words sent a shiver up my spine.

Grandpa entered first, crawling on his hands and knees, his large, naked body slowing as he wriggled through the tight entrance. Arthur's dad was next, followed by Watcher, Arthur, then me. I was awfully glad it was as dark as it was. I couldn't see anything, but I looked away just in case.

It was my job to pull the flap of buffalo skins down and tuck it around the base so not even a hint of light could enter the sweat lodge. I succeeded with hardly any help at all — a pitch-black sky didn't hurt none.

I sat next to the entrance, beside Arthur's dad, my head bent slightly forward by the curve of the roof. Arthur sat on the other side of the entrance across from me. Beside him sat Watcher. Grandpa sat at the far end of the pit.

The rocks glowed with a pale red light. The air was hot and the green branches around me smelled of tree sap and living leaves.

Arthur's dad moved his sweaty arm against mine as he searched for a comfortable position for sitting. There wasn't any in this part of the world.

All I could see was the glow from the rocks and the shape of knees jutting out toward the hot pit.

Grandpa's voice rose above the thunder as he called to the Great Spirit, in English. He called north and south and east and west. He called from above and from below.

A flame erupted from the rocks. In the flash of red, I saw them all. Arthur's eyes were squeezed tightly closed, his face wrinkled like an old man's. Watcher rocked back and forth as he sang in Blackfoot. Arthur's dad scooped handfuls of smoke and rubbed it over his face and neck. Grandpa took a pinch of powder from a bundle and flicked it at the rocks. The rocks sparked orange and yellow. He cupped his hand in a water bucket I had not noticed and poured a handful of water over the rocks. In a breath, the air was black again, filled with the smell of sage and damp earth and sweat.

Beside me, Arthur's dad's shoulder was jerking against my skin as if he was crying.

As Grandpa's voice rose, it grew quick and loud, shifting to mostly Blackfoot words that had feeling for me but no meaning. Then the English was gone completely, and I felt I was in a world that had become ancient and Indian.

His voice became heavy and thick. His words flowed without a break or a pause or even a breath, like he had become the spirit he had called upon.

A flame erupted from the pit, Grandpa's hand opened, and a cloud of steam crushed the fire.

Arthur tightly gripped the earth at the edge of the pit.

I reached across to touch Arthur, but a large hand clamped over my wrist and pushed me back. When I lifted my arm to my lips, I felt the fine powder that had been on Grandpa's fingers. My lips tingled, then became numb, as if all my blood had suddenly drained out.

The words were still strange, but they left in me images I had never seen or could have even made up: I was riding a wild mustang across the prairie grass, chasing a herd of buffalo. Around me were a dozen Blackfoot warriors not much older than me. We cut and turned, dust rising in the thunder of hooves, as we pushed the buffalo into the narrowing trap. When one last buffalo had been forced inside, the stragglers turned and ran. The warriors tore off their clothes and ran naked across the backs of the enclosed buffalo.

A red fire erupted from the rocks. A white cloud rose from the pit. All around, the air smelled of animal.

Watcher called out in a mix of Blackfoot and English.

"Great Spirit," he said, "help my father find a way out of the darkness of alcohol."

Grandpa answered in his continuous, heavy voice.

A rock flashed with a bluish color.

Now the air smelled of an old woman's home, full of sickness and loss.

A lump of hot earth struck me hard on the chest. I clamped my hand over the scar. A second lump hit the back of my hand.

"I want to be a man," Arthur said, and hurled a third piece of earth at my scar. "What do I have to do to earn my place? Give me a chance to be an Indian."

It seemed my turn had come.

I repeated Arthur's words exactly as if they were my own.

Again the rocks glowed with the powder that made blue light, but now the air smelled of something that made me turn away. It was gunpowder, that heavy acid that burns the back of the throat like poison gas.

If Arthur's dad spoke, I never heard his voice above the sound of the thunder booming over our heads. The ground shook with such fury the sweat was knocked from my skin. Then came the wind and the rain and the hail, worse than I had ever dreamed, beating the buffalo robes with the vengeance of all the Indian spirits in all the heavens, as if now was the time for all the years of the white man's lies to be driven from the land.

I pushed my hands over my head and held the boughs of the sweat lodge as it pulled against the earth.

The fold of buffalo robe jerked open, a wind whipped driving sleet inside. A face appeared in the opening and

MURDER ON THE RIDGE

stared at me, then at Arthur. He wore a metal pan hat and army uniform.

"Damn this army," he said. "They've sent children to fight."

He dropped the flap, half covering the opening, and disappeared into the sleet and the rumble of heavy guns and rattle of machine-gun fire.

It Was Just Dead

The cold air whipped the flap of the sweat lodge, slapping the bent sticks that formed the roof and walls. It was empty except for me and Arthur.

"What's that stink?" I asked.

Arthur's eyes jerked from side to side, then stared at the spot where the buffalo robes touched the ground.

There, behind where Grandpa had been sitting, was a dead rat, its lips pulled back over its teeth like it was warning us to keep away, its bloated body looking ready to explode.

"I'm gettin' outta here," Arthur said.

"Where're you going?"

"I'll know when I get there."

"I'm waiting for the others to get back."

"They're not coming back."

"How do you know that?"

"Because they didn't go anywhere." He reached outside to the stack of clothes he'd put beside the sweat lodge, set them between his knees and stared down at the pale green woolen pants, the army shirt and the metal pan helmet. "It's us who've gone somewhere."

"Don't be stupid, Arthur."

"Go on, stick your head out into that sleet and see for yourself."

"It's just some kind of weird hail or something. Those clothes belong to somebody else. Yours are out there somewhere. And I don't plan to go out and get wet and cold."

"Well, I am going." He got dressed and hooked his belt. "You know who that soldier was?"

"Don't leave me here alone."

"It was Wolfleg."

I knew it. I just didn't want to admit it. If I did, it would mean Arthur and I were having the same dream with the same people and talking to each other about the same things. That just didn't happen in dreams. So it had to mean this was something far worse than dreaming.

"I think we're on Vimy Ridge," Arthur said. "And that thunder is our big guns pounding the German trenches. I think that man was Wolfleg. And if we don't do something, he's going to get killed today. Just like the book in the Grayson Library said."

"I think there was something in that crazy smoke," I said. "I think it's making us see things."

Arthur reached over and slapped my face.

"What was that for?"

"To show you this is real. It's not a dream. And it's not Grandpa's crazy Indian smoke."

All over my body, my sweat had frozen to my skin. I began to shake. When I tried to talk, my voice broke and I started to cry.

"I'm not going out there." I tried to swallow. "I don't want to die."

He slapped my face with his other hand.

I stared at the dead rat while Arthur crawled out into the sleet storm that whipped Vimy Ridge on that Easter morning in 1917, when a battle made Canada a real country and killed Wilfred Black.

A hard gust hit the flap with such force that it got hooked on a jagged piece of branch hanging from the ceiling. The wind would have frozen me right on the spot if a heat hadn't risen in me like the rot working inside the dead rat. I half expected it to roll over onto its fat, bloated belly and walk out into the storm, like Arthur had just done. But now it didn't seem to be warning me. It seemed to have no expression at all, it was just dead, like nothing mattered at all in this world.

Arthur stuck his head in and dropped a pile of clothes at my side.

"I found these over by that tree where you undressed," he said. "Only it's not a tree anymore. It's a bunch of half-drunk Canadians hollering and cussing about waiting too long to kill the Hun."

He disappeared, then reappeared a second later and set Grandpa's rubber boots, with the dry wool socks inside, next to my clothes.

"A guy with a handlebar mustache tried to stick a bayonet between my ribs, just to get these dry boots," he said.

"What's happening, Arthur?" I asked, trying not to let my lips quiver. "Why are we here?"

"Because you asked to come here," he said. "Just like I did. And because you think *this* makes you so darned brave." He poked me hard on my jagged scar.

I rubbed my hand over the spot.

Arthur cussed and moved out into the storm.

"What are you going to do?" I asked as I dressed.

"The same thing you're going to do."

Arthur had prayed for what he'd wanted, and I had copied his prayer, repeating his exact words. Though I didn't know why I did it or that I was even doing it, I did know I regretted saying Arthur's prayer. I wanted to think it just happened by accident, because I usually said the wrong thing at the wrong time. But I was afraid that maybe something else was talking for me. Still, I wasn't going up Vimy Ridge. I'd read too much about the war to be that stupid.

"We're not going to find out who killed Wolfleg," Arthur said. "We're going to stop it from happening. If I have to pull the trigger myself, I'll do it. We'll stop thirty-five years of hatred and misery before it starts. If we do, we'll change Grayson."

I wished I could give Arthur the scar he wanted, the one he deserved. I'd tear it from my flesh if he wouldn't have to go out into the storm and up Vimy Ridge in the face of an enemy who had already killed more Frenchmen and Englishmen than were in the whole Canadian army two times over.

Put Me up Front, Cap

I crawled out of the sweat lodge and stood in a depression in the earth, my back to the driving sleet. The trench twisted a short distance along the ridge, then flared out into the mouth of a giant crater. Hundreds of men crouched behind the steep forward slope. At the back of the crater, Arthur stood with a platoon of soldiers, most carrying small bombs and machine guns, a few with long Lee-Enfield rifles. Arthur lifted a large tin cup. As he took a drink, he choked. For a minute, it looked like he was going to throw up.

One of the soldiers hit him on the back. "If you can't handle it, lad," he said, his words all slurred, "I'll do my damnedest to help you out."

Arthur waved him away. He bent over, holding on to one knee. He took another drink, more like a sip, and let out another barrage of gagging and choking.

"This tastes like turpentine," Arthur finally said, and wiped his sleeve across his lips.

"Army rum'll cut more than paint," the soldier said. "It'll cut the heart out of a coward."

"Give me another," a second soldier said. "I must be

getting a bit nervous."

"Nervous?" a third asked. "Loewan here just filled his pants with a load that'll kill more Huns than mustard gas."

The wind and sleet battered the backs of the men. As Arthur handed the tin cup to the first man, I saw Albert Loewan stare out into the storm. In my time, in 1952, Loewan worked as Old Man Howe's foreman, doing Howe's dirty work and some of his own. But he was so young, hardly eighteen that day, when the Battle of Vimy Ridge was fought. I never saw such fear in a man's eyes, a searching stare, looking for a place to hide, someplace where death wouldn't find him. For a second, I felt sorry for him. I even considered walking up and telling him that he made it through the Battle of Vimy Ridge, even the whole war. But when I remembered the hateful man he'd become, I decided to let him find out on his own.

Then I glanced quickly to see if there was a place for me to hide. There wasn't.

Arthur worked his way toward me through the mud and sleet, his arm up to protect his face.

I met him halfway.

"We're going up first," Arthur said into the storm, his breath thick with rum. "We'll hug the artillery barrage all the way to the top. Wilfred Black is in our company. I didn't see him or Pots or Warren. But I figure they got to be here."

As I huddled with my shoulders shrugged up

against the wind, I thought of the story I'd read in the history book in the Grayson library, how the soldiers following the Creeping Barrage could get killed by their own artillery, how Pots and Warren, Loewan and Wolfleg had all been on Vimy Ridge following the barrage, and all but Wilfred Black, Wolfleg, came back.

"I ain't going," I said.

"Doesn't that scar mean anything?"

"It was a mistake. That's all I ever said it was."

"Well, you don't have a choice," he said. "You put on that uniform like I did, like all the others did, even manure-in-his-pants Loewan."

"You, men!" a voice called. "Who wants a kick at the Hun?"

"I, Cap!" they called.

"Who's too drunk to fight?"

"Not I, Cap!" they called together.

"Any man who's too drunk, I want him up front, where he can't shoot me in the back. I want the Creeping Barrage biting at his hide."

"I'm too drunk!" they called in a single voice. "Put me up front, Cap!"

"Leave room for me!" the captain called back. "You men hold the Hun down, and I'll kick his ass!"

A roar rose above the wind and the sleet and the rumble of guns and the rattle of machine guns.

Then the guns fell silent, and in the growing dawn, Cap held up five fingers as he checked his watch. He drew his bayonet and fixed it to his rifle barrel, and all up the trenches and around the craters, the dawn air clicked metal on metal. When he held four fingers out, the gas-filled shells fired from the rear. At three minutes to go, a shape appeared on the ridge of the crater, set a football in the mud and kicked it over the German trenches.

Cap clenched his fingers into a tight fist.

The Canadian artillery opened fire with a thunderous barrage, shaking all the earth, flashing red and orange in the Easter Monday morning air. The captain hollered, but no one heard him. When his arm lowered toward the ridge, we climbed over the rim of the giant crater and moved forward, the sleet stinging our cheeks, the mud sucking at our feet as we hunched under our packs, walking slowly, like we didn't have a worry in the world, toward what white history would call Canada's coming of age and the Blackfoot would call murder on the ridge.

Shot for Cowardice

I'm not going. I said it over and over to myself, as if the words would make me stay put, leave that unholy mess to somebody else. But I went anyway.

Then, as if the captain had heard my thoughts, he held up his hand, stopping our advance. We all stood in the mud with the sleet cutting through the air. On my left, Canadian soldiers poured from a tunnel opening into the far side of the giant crater. Directly ahead of us, the flat snaking German trench shook with the sound of explosions beneath its surface. The trench bulged from the face of the ridge like a great mouth. Water, and mud, and running rats flowed toward us. Cap's face twisted as he screamed the order. I dropped facedown into the chalk and muck. The ground lifted under me, jerked me backward down the slope. The trench exploded in a blaze of orange light. Barbed wire fell in long twisting lines behind us. Chunks of jagged wooden planking rained down, stabbing at the ground.

Something hot stung my right shoulder.

Ahead, the German trenches had become a gaping

hole a hundred feet across and too deep for men in the hurry of battle to cross.

Cap rose and waved us forward.

I rolled off my injured shoulder and turned, facing the soldier who'd given Arthur the rum. His face was turned slightly to mine. His eyes were open, with not a care in this world. He was no longer breathing, but I could still smell the rum.

Three others from our platoon didn't stand to follow Cap up the ridge.

"Don't look," Arthur said as we stepped over them.

I slipped my hand under my tunic and rubbed my shoulder. The stinging was gone. Now it just felt numb. Under my touch, a hot curved piece of metal jutted out from my flesh. I jerked it, but my fingertips slipped from its damp, bloody surface.

Thirty feet ahead, to our right, men dropped to their bellies, crept to the trench and tossed their small round bombs over the edge. Water and mud erupted in narrow columns. Men poured into the trenches like they'd been carried along by an invisible river.

Voices cussed.

Machine-gun fire rattled.

Men heaved themselves from the trenches and hunched over up the ridge just out of reach of the Creeping Barrage.

We crossed down the top edge of the crater and stepped through the mud and debris that marked the German trench.

Among the lumps of crumbled earth at the bottom of the trench, a soldier worked over a delirious wounded man.

"Get the savage off me!" the man called out and cussed. "He's takin' my arm!"

The medic hollered to a shape sitting at the back of the trench. "Help me here! The arm is gone, but we can save his life!"

The sitting man lifted his head from his knees, his face as white as chalk. "I'm not going out there," the man said. "Let the drunken fool go to hell. Nobody'll miss him."

"I'll have you shot for cowardice."

The sitting man set his rifle between his knees. "You're lucky Clarence Howe didn't come himself," he said as the artillery roared. "Or you'd already be dead."

"What did you say?"

"I ain't goin' out there, Indian!"

Arthur took a few quick steps toward the group. The sitting man jerked toward Arthur and pointed his rifle.

"I'll help," Arthur said.

I stood frozen in the driving sleet, the thunder of guns swallowing the human voices. But I would have known them all even if I hadn't seen their features in the dim light and the flashes of cannon fire.

"Wolfleg," I thought I heard Arthur say, "I didn't know you were a medic. Tell me what to do."

The sitting man was Pots. My mom called him the Gray-haired Bully. Dad called him the Cheat. And the

Blackfoot people called him *Kaxtomo*, the Enemy.

The wounded man was Joe Warren, a man I called Singing Man, the one-armed drunk who lived in a room above the Grayson beer parlor. One of the most hateful men who ever lived.

As I stood and watched Wilfred work on Warren, him so drunk and wounded he didn't know what was real, I remembered the story everyone in Grayson knew. How Pots had save Joe Warren's life that day on Vimy Ridge. How he would have died if not for Pots. How Pots, as he told it, "removed the dead arm to save his life." And now I watched Pots's lie.

Arthur followed each order Wilfred gave, reaching for this bandage, cutting this cloth, pressing on that pulsing artery, as if he had been trained. When Wilfred finished, he stood and slung his medic pack over his shoulder.

"I've got work to do," he said, turning to go.

In the growing light, I could see the Lee-Enfield follow Wilfred's tall back. When Pots's finger moved around the trigger, I jumped toward him.

"Murderer!" I hollered into the thunder of artillery.

Wilfred jerked his head around, his eyes moving from me to Pots. Arthur sprung from his crouch toward the back of Wilfred's long legs. Pots's right arm snapped back as the Lee-Enfield recoiled between his upright knees.

Wilfred's medical pack oozed a dark fluid. When Arthur caught his legs, Wilfred was already falling.

Now I had both hands on the rifle. Pots drove his

elbow into the side of my face, but I jerked the rifle from his grip and slammed the brass butt plate across the bridge of his nose as Arthur called out a mournful cry in Blackfoot and rose from Wilfred's side.

The next second, Arthur was standing over Pots with the machine gun Warren had carried.

"No, Arthur!" I cried.

Arthur didn't tell me to mind my own business, or even turn a hundred years of white hatred of Indians back on me. He did nothing but squeeze the trigger. The machine gun pulsed in his hands. Bullets exploded against the back of the trench. Pots jumped for cover but was struck hard. As he lay motionless in the sleet and mud, I thought I saw Arthur smile.

Wounded Soldiers

The sleet was gone. The wind was gone. And the air felt too warm for Vimy Ridge. But inside, I felt as cold as if someone had opened me up and set my heart out on the wind-driven ridge. It made me feel sick what Pots had done, but the feeling that cut out my heart was the sight of Arthur doing the same, that maybe he was no different from Pots.

I had my cheekbones resting on my upright knees and my arms protecting my head, willing myself away from the mud and the sleet and the death. I felt a big hand on my shoulder shaking me, and realized I was crying.

"Sapanistsim."

I lifted my head into the dim yellow light of a coal-oil lantern on the ground outside the sweat lodge. A big Indian was staring at me, holding the buffalo-robe flap open.

"What?"

"Sapanistsim," he said again. "Is complete."

"I don't understand."

"Sweat is complete. Time to go to bed."

I stared across the pit of cold sweat-lodge rocks at Arthur staring back at me.

"You shouldn't've done it, Arthur."

"It was a dream."

"But you said it was real."

He didn't answer, just crawled out from under the flap of buffalo robes Grandpa had dropped closed. When I followed, he was already half dressed.

I suppose I expected Arthur to defend himself, to say Pots had it coming, that at least Pots was gone, and even if we didn't save Wilfred, at least Grayson would be different.

But he just cinched his belt and turned away.

"If it wasn't real, why'd we go? Why'd we bother?"

Arthur didn't turn.

"And why do I feel dead inside?"

Arthur took one long, quick stride toward me. He slapped me so hard across the face the force spun me around and I fell into the tall grass and brush lining the trail. For a second, I thought I heard a thunderclap, that I was back on Vimy Ridge. I reached out for the trench and caught a handful of chokecherries. I lay there looking up into the night sky, stinging from Arthur's hand.

Somewhere out in the darkness, Arthur was fighting a sound he could not control, the quiet crying that comes from such a deep place it seems very old.

As I lay there, the yellow glow of the coal-oil light stopped at my outstretched feet. Grandpa's face leaned forward through the chokecherry bush and stared at me. Then he put his big hand behind my back and pulled me up until I felt myself fall across his shoulder like a small child.

He ran his hand up my arm to my shoulder, following the trail of blood that had now dried on my skin. Then he turned the light to Arthur on the opposite side of the path.

"Wounded soldiers," he said. "Too old to carry both. Have to make two trips."

He draped my uninjured arm around his neck and cradled his own under my legs. As he walked, his body felt warm. He smelled of clean, new sweat and wood smoke from a campfire.

"Lots of thunder. Too much lightning. Hail like sweat-lodge rocks," he said. "Big battle with many white men."

"Yes," I said, too tired to hold my eyes open.

My head bumped into Grandpa's shoulder. I jerked myself awake and thought I saw Arthur walking up the path behind us. He seemed to be carrying something. My clothes. I let my head rest easy on Grandpa's wide shoulder, the smell of the olden-days Indian filling my mind with images and memories I knew weren't mine. I wasn't asleep, but still I couldn't form the words I wanted to ask. Did you ever kill a man? Maybe it was because he was the kind of man he was, someone who talked to spirits, but he seemed to hear my thoughts.

Killing is easy, I thought I heard him say. It's living with it that torments the soul.

Damn You Men and Your Sweat Lodge

When we got back to camp, my arm felt like it was on fire, and I was shivering so bad I thought I must've caught something from the rats. Then I felt the heat of the campfire, and warm blankets being wrapped around me. And inside it all, I heard Arthur's mom.

"How long was he out there?"

Grandpa said something I didn't understand.

"An hour?" she said. "This wound is at least two days old."

Grandpa leaned over and touched my face with the back of his large hand. Again, he spoke in Blackfoot.

"Damn you," Arthur's mom said. "Damn you men and your sweat lodge."

Grandpa kept on whispering in my ear, as if he hadn't heard her. But she was as angry as I'd ever seen. She spoke in coarse rough words to Arthur's dad and Watcher, then glared at them when they just stared at her.

"I need medicine plants," she said, shooing them. "From the woods. Go get them. Now!"

They stood suddenly, like boys in trouble, and headed off into the woods as Arthur appeared.

She checked her son for injuries, but when she didn't find any visible ones, she took a long knife from her cooking box and shoved the blade into the hot embers. Then she turned back to me.

"There's something bad in you," she said. "I'll have to cut it out."

In the darkness, I could see Arthur disappear into the night, following the men to the woods.

"Okay," she said, "hold him still."

Grandpa's Blackfoot words rolled toward me like they had in the sweat lodge, and I knew what they meant even if I couldn't understand them.

As he placed his hand over the jagged scar running down my left breast, I could smell burning flesh. I felt no pain, no sting, no heat, nothing, just the pressure of Grandpa's hand and the sound of his ancient voice.

Arthur's mom leaned toward the firelight and turned something in her fingertips.

"It's a metal button," she said. "It's got thread on it and some cloth from a heavy coat. It's got markings that aren't from this time."

She turned back to Grandpa.

"Where was this boy?" she asked.

"The Great White War."

I heard him say those words as fever rolled my eyes back, as I could feel the heat of my own breath. The blankets became tight and heavy across my chest. Then I was lifted into the air, only to have memory return me to the rats and sleet and mud-covered ridge.

Back with the Living

When I woke, I could hear strange-sounding voices. I tried to move, but that made the wound in my shoulder sting more than I could stand. I lay there for a long time with my eyes closed, not wanting to see where I was.

"Septic?" my dad's voice said. "I suppose that means something to a doctor."

"An infection." It was Dr. Wilcox. "It often follows a wound left untreated for several days."

"Several days? Mom saw the boy half naked Sunday morning. He was fine then. It's that damned Indian medicine they smeared on him. That's what made him sick."

"That Indian medicine quite likely saved his arm if not his life."

"It nearly killed him."

"Jim," Mom said, "please let the doctor speak."

"Why does he have to hang around with Indians all the time? I don't understand that."

"Jim," Mom said softly.

"Okay, but I don't know why he can't have some white friends."

I caught a sudden smell of chlorine gas and jerked my head away before I realized it was just bleach — somebody had probably cleaned a toilet bowl. I took an easy breath. Even if I hadn't seen the picture of the young queen hanging on the wall, I'd have known I was in the Indian hospital.

Mom and Dad and Dr. Wilcox were standing together in the far corner of the room. I had to move my legs under the covers and make a low coughing sound to get somebody to look my way.

"Good Lord." Dad nearly knocked Mom over when he nudged her. "He's back with the living."

Before I could make another sound, Mom had her arms around me and was kissing me all over my face and neck and head.

"My baby," she said over and over, crying big tears.

"Mom, you're making me all wet."

"A smart remark." She showered me with more kisses. "Now I know my baby's back."

Before Mom could get out of the way, Dad was at it, too. He wasn't trying to kiss me or anything stupid like that, but he did give my head a good rub with the flat of his hand, as if he was knocking some dust off something he liked. When I saw the stern look on his face, I knew I'd have trouble lying my way out of this one.

"Where's Arthur?" I asked Mom when Dad turned back to Dr. Wilcox.

"He's outside with his family. They've been here nearly the whole time."

"I guess that's quite a while."

"Over two days since they brought you in."

"Two days?"

Dad and Dr. Wilcox glanced over at me, then went back to talking. It seemed to be awfully important judging by all the whispering.

"We thought we were going to lose you," she said. Her eyes filled with tears.

I was afraid she'd start kissing me all over again.

"They brought me in the dark?" I asked quickly. "All the way from Horse Shoe Backwater?"

"Yes," Mom said. "It nearly killed those poor old horses."

"Better them than me."

Mom lifted her hand to give me a swat, checked which shoulder was hurt and slapped me across the other.

"Ouch, what was that for?"

"I don't know," Mom said. "You're a boy, so there's bound to be something."

I could tell Mom was feeling better, but once she found out the truth about what had happened to me, there'd be a good deal more swatting to duck. Mom was kind of religious — not in the sense that Arthur's grandpa was, Mom was more church religious. Right now I wasn't sure who was right about God, but I did know lying wasn't going to get me anything but trouble. I also knew I didn't want either god mad at me and get sent to hell or back to Vimy Ridge.

The door opened and a nurse came in, pushing a cart with smells coming off it as good as anything I'd smelled in life.

"Breakfast," she said. "Word is you're alive and hungry enough to eat hospital food."

People like to joke about how bad hospital food is, but I'd been in this one to visit Yellowfly after he got beat up. He wasn't very hungry one time, and I got to eat pretty much the whole meal, except the Jell-O. Yellowfly liked Jell-O. Generally the food was pretty good — the only thing about it that got me worried was if there was enough of it.

When I glanced over to where Dr. Wilcox and Dad had been talking, they were both gone.

Mom was busy lifting this lid and checking that plate and stirring milk into the porridge, then sprinkling brown sugar over the steam rising from the bowl, all the time looking at me for a sign that she was putting on just the perfect amount. Then the door opened again, and Dr. Wilcox stood holding it like a gentleman. The nurse left without a word, but Mom didn't notice him until he cleared his throat.

"Well," she said, "you could just ask me to leave."

"Okay, I need a minute alone with the boy."

Mom kissed my forehead, scowled at Dr. Wilcox and walked out into the hallway.

Dr. Wilcox pulled the chrome-legged chair to the side of my bed, sat, crossed his legs and stared at me as if to figure out who I was.

"I want to know what happened," he finally said. "I've already talked to your friend Arthur, so you won't get away with lying to me."

I told him everything, just as it had happened.

"God help us," he said, and patted my knee. "You eat. I've got to talk to your dad."

"You believe me?"

"No," he said. "But it's the same story Arthur told, and I believe you believe it."

"You think Arthur's grandpa tricked me?"

"I believe he also believes it."

"Why can't you?"

"I'm a scientist," he said. "Science needs proof. Something we can measure and analyze."

"Can't you just believe it's true?"

"Have faith?"

"I saw you in church."

He grinned. "Don't confuse going to church with anything resembling faith."

"You said 'God help us.'"

He'd been a doctor in the Second World War. I believed he knew way more misery than I'd seen on Vimy Ridge.

"That button isn't something you see every day," he said. "It came from a German officer in the Great War, from his long coat. How did it get buried in you? It must have been moving at terrific speed."

He went to the window and put his hands on his hips. I thought maybe he was just staring out at nothing, but I saw him glance down at where I figured Arthur's family was waiting.

"Hell," he said, turning back to me. "How do you get a button moving that fast? It was like it was shot from a gun."

I thought about the explosion that lifted the whole German trench, forcing a bulge in the earth, then the orange flash, the stinging in my shoulder, and the wood and mud and rats and maybe even Germans raining down on the soldiers.

"I'm going to talk to your dad," he said, and left.

I put my hand over the wound in my shoulder. Though the pain had passed, I could still feel that heat inside me. I wondered if part of a German was in me now.

The sound of voices speaking quietly and calmly turned into a loud shout and a burst of cusses. The door flew open and Dad came stomping in. His face was red and his eyes were hard and dark.

"For God's sake, boy," he said, "can't you think of a better story?"

"It's not a story."

"Shut up," Dad said. "You won't tell it again, do you hear me? Your mom can't hear some crazy Indian story. Nobody can. They'll run her out of the church she's been fighting to get respect from her whole life."

"You want me to lie?"

"Yes, dammit."

"What should I say?"

"Think of something," Dad said. "You're good at lying."

"I'm not lying."

He moved quickly toward me.

I turned my face away from the blow I knew was coming. I had my eyes closed a minute later when he still hadn't hit me. When I finally opened them, he was sitting on the chair that Dr. Wilcox had sat in, his face resting in his cupped hands.

"I didn't say you were."

"You believe me?"

He looked up at me, his face as kind as I could remember.

"Yes."

He seemed to be a man I'd never known before, someone who'd seen things as inhuman as the Great White War, yet had never been there.

Nobody Waved

I lay there for a while expecting somebody to come into the room and start kissing me or give my head a good rub or bring me more food. When nobody came, my shoulder started to hurt. Pretty soon, I was feeling sorry for myself.

I stared at the picture of our new queen on the far wall. She was young and pretty, more like a teacher fresh from teachers' school than somebody who'd order men to die in a war.

In the corner of the ceiling was a brown stain like something had got spilled and leaked down through to my room. A few feet farther to the right and the queen would be sending me to fetch her a towel. I could do that, but I didn't think I could go to war for her, if she had one.

I pushed the breakfast cart aside and stood. I felt weak and a little wobbly, but at least I wasn't burning up inside with the heat of a long-ago war and the fear and anger and regret of a long-dead German officer trying to get me to join him in the grave.

I wanted to go home.

I rubbed the bandage taped over my wounded shoulder and walked over to the window. It looked out to the road heading south to Heavy Shield School.

Dad was talking to Grandpa and Arthur's father. Arthur was sitting on the grass near the horses, looking like he was ready to fall asleep. Arthur's mom and my mom were sitting in our old pickup. I couldn't tell for sure if they were talking because I could only see the backs of their heads, but they probably were. And I'd bet it was about their kids. Moms always talk about their kids first, then they go on to cooking and cleaning, and finally finish with something nice about their husbands.

My dad only had two ways of talking to other men — he was either laughing and joking or he was hollering and cussing, which meant there'd soon be either a good deal of drinking or a good deal of fighting.

But today was different. Grandpa spoke and my dad and Arthur's dad nodded. Arthur's dad spoke and Grandpa and my dad nodded. Then my dad spoke and Grandpa and Arthur's dad nodded. Then they just stood, like they were thinking about something important — probably about how I shouldn't be talking about things that went on in an Indian sweat lodge. Then Grandpa called out and waved to Arthur's mom and then to Arthur.

A few minutes later, they were all on the wagon heading down the road.

Dad stood with Mom.

Nobody waved.

I watched until the wagon was out of sight. I wondered if Arthur was thinking about me. I wondered if
he knew what had been said among the men, if we'd
have to sneak around to be friends. Ever since I woke
up, I'd been expecting Arthur to come walking
through my door with a smart grin on his face, give
me an elbow in the ribs and tease me about something
I did that made me look like I'd never learn enough to
be an Indian. But Arthur wasn't coming.

I went back to bed, pulled the covers up to my chin
and fell asleep with the image of Arthur firing the
machine gun until not a shell was left, until Pots lay
motionless at the bottom of the trench, and Arthur's
face twisted in pain as he cried silent tears under the
thunder of guns.

None of Us Can Change the Past

That night, after I'd eaten my supper and licked all the plates and bowls, Dr. Wilcox removed the tape from the top of my shoulder and folded the bandage down. I could tell that he wanted to poke the edge of the wound to see if he could get something to drain out, but he thought better of it.

He rubbed his chin instead.

"We'll see how it looks in the morning," he said. "But I wouldn't be surprised if you're home by midday."

"I feel pretty good."

"You must be getting tired of our food."

"It's okay. There's just not enough."

"Not enough hospital food? You must be feeling better."

He retaped the bandage and wiped his hands on a paper towel.

"I want you to avoid sweat lodges for the next few weeks. At least until your shoulder is completely healed."

"I don't plan to go back ever again."

"You're a wise lad."

He crumpled the paper towel and dropped it into the garbage can, pushed open the door and paused for a few long seconds.

"None of us can change the past," he finally said. "What's done is done. The most we can hope for is to forgive and forget." He glanced at our young queen hanging on the wall. "Go to sleep now," he said, then disappeared into the hallway.

I did my best, but I couldn't sleep. Maybe I was slept out, or maybe it was because I kept thinking about Arthur.

Just before midnight, I jerked upright to the *tick tick* sound of something hitting my window. I got out of bed and peered around the corner of the curtain.

Arthur stood in the light cast by the lamp above the main entrance.

When I moved into clear view, he waved me down. I waved him up.

He shook his head and shrugged.

I took the gray wool blanket from the bed and draped it over my shoulders like an old-time Indian. I worked my way down the long hallway to the fire stairs leading out the back of the building. Arthur was waiting for me in the shadows, halfway to the line of tall poplars bordering the hospital grounds.

The air was cool and I felt a slight shiver. I pulled the blanket close to my chin and stepped across the gravel in my bare feet. In the dim light, he seemed odd to me, not the grinning smart guy I'd seen nearly every day since we were both six years old. His eyes looked sad, like taking Pots's life had also taken part of his own.

In his hand was a pair of old work boots.

"Who are those for?" I asked.

"I never told anybody what I did," Arthur said, ignoring my question. "It's been three days. I can hardly sleep. I haven't heard anybody say Pots's name. It's like he never existed."

Arthur tipped his head toward the grass and the tall poplars. "Let's get outta sight."

I followed Arthur across the dewy grass, our breath making little clouds in the late August air. Once we were at a safe distance, Arthur held out the boots. They were very big, like the ones I'd seen Grandpa wear.

"Put these on."

"Why?"

"I gotta find out about Pots."

"Now?" I said. "I don't think I'm supposed to leave the hospital."

"You just did."

"I know that, but I can go back inside in a few seconds."

"Please, Will" — Arthur handed me the boots — "I gotta know if I'm —"

He stopped short of saying "a killer" or "a murderer" or "just like Pots," or whatever he thought he had become. I took the boots, but not because I hadn't heard anything about Pots. It was because Arthur had said please, which was something he'd never done before. And there was another reason. Arthur seemed to have lost his spirit. He seemed not to be an Indian anymore.

"Okay," I said. "But I'm not going to be able to run with Grandpa's boots on." I sat and laced them. "How come you didn't bring some clothes? This blanket makes me look like an Indian."

"One of us has to."

I knotted the blanket around my neck, then tied the thick string from my hospital gown around my waist.

"You're not going to hit me again, are you?"

"No," Arthur said. "Not unless you keep asking stupid questions."

"Hi, Arthur." I stuck out my hand.

"What's that for?"

"It's nice to see you again."

"I've been here for the last ten minutes."

"No you haven't," I said. "You just got back when you made that smart remark."

"Let's get going. We don't have all night."

The real Arthur, my friend was trying to come back, but I was afraid of what we'd find in town, and that it would drive him away forever.

We Shouldn't've Come

The cool night air had put all the insects to sleep. I didn't mind that there were no mosquitoes, but the quiet was making me nervous, kind of like when all the guns went silent just before the battle for Vimy Ridge. Though I'd slept for over two days, I felt worn down to nothing. My feet were heavy, and my legs ached from dragging Grandpa's big boots all the way to town.

Arthur and I stood on the sidewalk lining Main Street opposite what had been Pots's insurance business. The big picture window where Pots liked to sit and look out over the town was boarded up.

"Oh, jeez," Arthur said, "I really killed him."

"Come on, Arthur, it's a boarded-up window. That doesn't mean anything except somebody had some extra boards."

I held the wool blanket tight to my body and started across the street, quickly, so Arthur would think it was okay to follow me, that nothing was different in Grayson just because there were boards covering a window. But when I got close enough to see there was no glass behind the boards, my nerve left me.

"It's empty," Arthur whispered over my shoulder. "There's no desk or chair or nothing. It's bare empty, like there never was anything inside."

We stood, staring at the building.

"We shouldn't've come."

"You can stand here if that's what you want," I said. "But I'm going to take a good look if I have to pry a board off."

When I peered inside, I saw Arthur was right. It was as empty as a bombed-out trench.

"This doesn't mean anything," I said. "I'm going to his house and I'll knock on his door until he wakes up or blows a hole through the door with his shotgun."

"It's over," Arthur said.

"You said you had to know. You dragged me outta my hospital bed. You dragged me up that darn ridge."

"I'm going home," he said.

I jerked my arm from under the wool blanket and slapped Arthur across the face, quick, but not strong.

Arthur just stood there, staring at me, with big tears rolling down his cheeks. I let my hands fall to my sides, giving him an easy shot if he wanted to take it, but he didn't do anything except hold his arms out to steady his body as he swayed, then sat roughly on the sidewalk.

I felt my blood turn hot inside, like the poison of Vimy Ridge was still in me. One of the meanest men I'd ever known was likely gone from this world forever, with not a soul to cry for him. But if the world was so much better off without him, why did I feel so miserable? Why did Arthur have to suffer when all he really wanted was justice?

A Ripe Crop of Fresh Pimples

I had seen the Mountie's car head the long way around town so he could sneak up on Indians trying to get beer from the drunken whites in the back of the beer parlor. But I guess he couldn't catch any bootlegging whites or Indians with illegal liquor because he rolled right up to me and Arthur.

He stuck his head out the window.

"What are you two doing?"

"Bugger off, flatfoot," Arthur said. He had a look on his face like when he shot Pots.

The Mountie stepped out into the street. He was tall and thin and had a ripe crop of fresh pimples all over his face.

"Get up."

Arthur just sat there.

"Are you deaf?"

Arthur didn't move.

The Mountie made three quick steps, grabbed Arthur by the upper arm and jerked him to standing.

"I figured you'd wait more than three hours to return to the scene of the crime."

"Why don't you shoot me?" Arthur said. "That'll fix things for both of us."

"Shoot you?" the Mountie said. "For breaking a window?"

"I didn't break any window."

He turned the flashlight on Arthur's face then flicked it on me.

"Okay," he said, "so you're not the right Indian, but I bet I could get him to swear a complaint against you two anyway."

"Who?"

"If Roy Potter saw you outside his busted window," he said. "He'd give you that shot you're asking for."

"Roy Potter?" Arthur asked. "Who's that?"

"Mr. Potter. Where've you two been, on the moon?"

"Roy Potter is Pots's real name," I whispered.

"Pots?" Arthur said. "He's alive?"

The Mountie stood very still for a second before he spoke. "I figured the fellow in the blanket for the crazy one. I was mistaken. I want you two off the street, or I'll put you in storage with Pots's furniture."

Arthur had such a big grin on his face, I was afraid he might kiss the Mountie.

"Did you hear that?" Arthur said to me. "Some Indian busted Pots's window."

"Probably knew Pots."

"Come on, Injun." Arthur put his arm around my blanket. "I should be gettin' you back to the hospital before you give our Mountie friend here the smallpox."

"Smallpox?" The Mountie almost tripped over his feet stepping back.

"Yeah," Arthur said. "But you don't have to worry. Judging by your face, I'd say you've already got 'em."

The Mountie was still looking for something to say when we angled down Main Street, heading toward the library.

"Did you see his face? If you slapped him, his head would leak right off his shoulders."

"Oh, yuck, Arthur."

"Constable Pimple Face of the Royal Canadian Mounted Police."

"Constable Puss Face."

"Con-puss-table Joe Oozy Face of the Oily Canadian Mounted Pimples."

I laughed so hard I almost missed that he'd worked his name-calling down the whole Mountie line all the way back to Colonel Macleod.

"What do you think?" Arthur asked.

"'Bout what?"

He said something dirty about Colonel Macleod, something as dirty as I'd ever heard, and I'd been listening to my dad cuss for thirteen years. I considered Dad a champion cusser.

"You better hope there's no such thing as ghosts," I said, "or Colonel Macleod's ghost will be after you for that one."

"I'll say it to his face. And if I see the ghost of that fork-tongued Jerry Potts, I'll tell him what I think, too."

"You better say he was the best translator any Indian chief or white colonel ever had at a treaty signing, or you'll be the one talking with a fork tongue."

Arthur didn't hear a word. His mind and mouth were going from one crazy thought to another like there was nothing better in this world than just finding out you were not a murderer after all.

In the twenty minutes it took us to walk back to the hospital, I thought of nothing else except how good it felt to have the old Arthur back, even if his conversation was a little rude.

Once we reached the line of tall poplars at the back of the hospital buildings, Arthur pointed at the stars shimmering against the black dome. He moved his finger from each point of light until I saw the shapes he had outlined: two figures standing together like friends in the background of night.

Arthur spoke in Blackfoot and gave my good shoulder an easy slap. I placed my hand over the heat of Arthur's touch and watched him disappear into the night. When I looked back at the stars, I couldn't find the figures, but in the same place I saw the shape of an old Indian looking down on Earth.

I headed to the hospital's rear entrance and worked my way up the long, narrow stairs, down the hallway of fresh paste wax and to my room. I flopped down on the bed with the wool blanket still wrapped around my body and Grandpa's big boots hanging loose on my feet.

I was as tired as a soul could be. But my mind was alive with images of Arthur shooting Pots with the machine gun. I thought Pots had died, yet there he was, still alive. And here I was having almost died from a German button in my shoulder. Nothing made sense. Why should I have nearly died and Pots come out uninjured? I'd been cheated. Why had we even gone to Vimy Ridge? Why had Grandpa's prayers or the spirits or the sweat lodge smoke sent us if we couldn't do anything to change the past?

Do You Know What Destiny Is?

I woke early in the morning. My arm felt light, as if it was floating in the air, then something cold touched my chest. I opened my eyes and saw Dr. Wilcox standing over me with rubber tubes hanging from his ears.

"Sleep well?"

"Pretty good."

He glanced down at Grandpa's boots sticking out from under the blanket wrapped around my body. I felt like a mummy wearing work boots.

"Were you out last night?"

"I don't think so."

"Are you still having problems distinguishing between reality and fantasy?" he asked as he set his thumb on the tip of my chin, opened my mouth and stuck a thermometer under my tongue. "This is a hospital, not a sweat lodge. Reality is all around you. It shouldn't be that hard to recognize."

I would've tried to mumble an answer, but a bitter taste on the thermometer made my mouth fill up with spit, and I didn't want to drool and look like I'd caught rabies, or he'd keep me in the hospital forever.

"I'd give you a shot to settle down those vivid dreams you've been having, if one existed," Dr. Wilcox said. "I've never seen a patient wake up dressed like he was still in a dream."

He moved around the foot of the bed to my injured shoulder. I followed him with my head, my lips puckered out around the thermometer like I was sucking on a cigarette.

He turned down the bandage, pushed his reading glasses up the bridge of his nose and bent over at the waist, his nose all scrunched up like that would help him see.

I made a sound like I was trying to clear my throat.

"Go ahead. Take it out," Dr. Wilcox said. "I only use the thermometer to keep patients quiet."

I took out the thermometer and swallowed.

"You don't want to know my temperature?"

"I can tell it's okay."

"Does that mean I can go home?"

"Can't see why not. It looks like you've been out half the night anyway."

"It wasn't that long," I said. "Besides, it's boring in here unless you're really sick."

Dr. Wilcox retaped the bandage and moved back around the bottom of the bed to Grandpa's boots. He turned my right boot to the side and examined the heel, took a jackknife from his pants pocket and flicked something from the sole.

"Would you look at that." He was holding a small piece of metal to the light. "If I wasn't a man of science, I'd say this was a Lee-Enfield slug. And if I didn't know better, I'd say you've had one of those war dreams."

"Aw, it's just a .303," I said. "They're all over, like squashed gophers in June."

"Not this one," he said, and held it in front of my face. "This one's army issue. Used them in the Great War. I could probably find one if I had to, but odds of finding one in your boot heel are pretty slim."

I took the slug. I'd loaded the Lee-Enfield I carried up Vimy Ridge with ten others just like it, and so had Pots. How did Grandpa get an army-issue slug in the heel of his work boot? I had no answer that made sense. It kept coming back to what Arthur had said was in Grandpa's message, that he'd seen Wilfred Black die, that he knew who did it.

"I can't tell the difference," I said and handed it back to Dr. Wilcox.

He just shook his head. "It came from your boot."

"I probably stepped on it."

"You have an odd way of explaining events. One minute, you claim you were on Vimy Ridge, and the next you refuse to acknowledge this slug could have come from there."

I didn't say anything.

"Okay." Dr. Wilcox took his stethoscope from around his neck and turned the rubber tubes around his palm, then stuffed them into the pocket of his white doctor's coat. He pushed my legs aside and sat on the edge of the bed.

"Remember when Pots tried to knock your head off with a baseball bat?"

"He missed."

"Not by much. Another inch to the left and I'd be sitting on your gravestone for this conversation."

"You'd come by to visit even if I was dead?"

"I like to visit my uncooperative patients at their resting place," he said. "I was at the graveyard just last night visiting with a patient who was talking smart with me just before I went in to get his gall bladder."

"I'm not talking smart," I said. "Besides, there's nothing wrong with my gall bladder."

"I could find something."

I closed my eyes and rested my head against the pillow. He wasn't going to stop until he'd said what he'd come to say.

"Then," he continued, "there was that wound on your chest. Your mom told me that if I tried to stitch you up, you'd run away from home."

I didn't open my eyes.

He set his hand over the scar on my chest like Arthur's grandpa had done when I was sick with the fever from the German button in my shoulder.

"It's been a hell of a summer, if you think about it."

I know, I thought.

"It's like everything that's important has come to this point in time, from different directions, crossing right here." He put his finger in the middle of my chest. "Do you know what destiny is?"

His finger felt heavy over my heart.

"Sure," I said, opening my eyes. "That's when a fella gets something he doesn't want. Like going pike fishing and catching a sucker."

"Destiny isn't always a bad event," he said. "It's just the effect of our actions — they seem to lead to an outcome that somehow makes perfect sense, almost as if it were planned."

"I thought you were a scientist. Shouldn't you be talking about how this slug traveled so fast, for so long, and hit my boot in a way that makes sense from the way you found it?"

I lifted my foot behind his back as if I was showing him something important, but he just set his hand on my knee and eased my leg down until it was flat on the bed.

"You are just a boy," he said, "but you have made me question things that I had assumed were hard rules."

"Maybe you should go to church and sit up front."

He laughed. "If I did, would you sit with me?"

I closed my eyes again and thought about how the reverend had told Arthur not to come back to His church with the heathen Indian god still inside him.

"I don't think so."

Let's Go Home

Shortly after noon, I was sitting across from Dad in our old pickup halfway between town and our house. His forehead was sweaty and the creases between his eyes pulled his eyebrows so close together they nearly touched.

"Four hundred and fifty dollars," he said over the rumble of the engine. "I don't even have four dollars and fifty cents left at the end of the month. Where am I going to find that kind'a money?"

He was talking about how much he owed the hospital for keeping me from dying. I still had Howe's forty dollars in my pants pocket. I'd checked when the nurse brought my clothes so I could dress and go home. I didn't know for sure what to do with the money, but knew I couldn't give it to Dad.

I kept my eyes focused on the road. He didn't need me looking at him right now. That would just set him off. But I couldn't help thinking about Mom, that he'd told me not to tell her what had really happened.

"I'm not going to lie to Mom," I said, staring through the cracks in the windshield.

"You don't have to," Dad said. "I did it for you."

"But she'll still ask me."

Dad took a hand-rolled cigarette from between the plastic cover and the paper of the tobacco pouch.

"Hold the wheel," he said, and struck a match with his thumbnail.

He blew a long stream of smoke out the side window and picked a piece of tobacco off the tip of his tongue.

"Just tell her what I already told you to say," he said, and took the wheel.

"I was sleeping half the time. I can't remember."

He gave me a sideways look like he knew I was lying.

"You and Arthur broke open some shotgun shells. You dumped out the bird shot and reloaded with rocks and anything that looked heavy and hard."

"Why'd we do that?"

"So you could bring down a deer."

"With a button?"

"Dammit," Dad said. "I didn't tell her you were smart."

"And Arthur shot me?"

"Accidentally."

"I'm not going to say that!"

Dad hit the brakes so hard he killed the engine. I got my arms up in front of my face just as my rear end came off the seat. I hit the windshield with the flats of my arms and bounced back to sitting. The truck skidded hard to the right and the front tire dropped into the ditch. Dad reached across me and jerked the door open.

"Get out!"

"Why?"

"I said, get out!"

"I'm not going."

Dad grabbed my good shoulder and gave me a hard shove. My head banged into the door as it swung back to closed. I tumbled into the tall ditch grass as the truck engine rolled over and fired. Before I could run, a line of gravel shot out from under the tire and hit me square on the chest, knocking me back onto my rear end.

Dad tore off with the truck still in first gear. The engine roared so loud I thought it would throw a rod. He hardly got a hundred yards when he stomped on the brakes and the truck veered back to the ditch. My door swung open then closed, then open again, trying its hardest to latch. A second later, the truck stopped, and Dad's door flew open. He stood there staring at me as the truck rolled down the ditch bank and came to a stop at the barbed wire fence lining the south field.

"Damn you," he said. "You'll lie to me, but not to her."

He tossed his cigarette on the road and ground it into the dirt. I thought he was going to come after me, maybe kick me in the rear end all the way home, as if that would make me think better about my words in the future. He didn't do anything but stand there.

I worked my way up the ditch bank and stood, facing him.

"Why in damnation is that?" he said. "I've worked hard every day of my life, and all I get is lies. I just want you to listen to me once. Is that so hard? Do you think I'm a worthless old man, fit for nothing but whispers and dirty talk? Hell, you treat Indians better than me."

He turned from me and walked down into the ditch. He stood for a long minute, staring at our pickup, then he cussed and kicked the tailgate that had dropped open from all the bumping and skidding and crashing into the ditch.

He sat on the tailgate and stared down the road at me.

I'd never seen Dad get so mad and not come after me with his belt swinging. Maybe he couldn't see any use in chasing somebody who could outrun him. Or maybe he'd just given up trying. Even though I didn't like getting a whupping, it was hard to see him like this.

I walked to the pickup and stopped at the ditch bank. "You want me to sit beside you?"

He shrugged. "It's a big tailgate."

I sat on the far right end nearest the license plate hanging at an angle from the taillight. Dad didn't even try to kick me or take a swing at me as I passed. I was worried that maybe he'd died with his eyes open, but then he pulled the tobacco pouch from his pocket and rolled a cigarette. He stared at the paper, with the strings of tobacco hanging out both ends.

"What I wouldn't give for a tailor-made," he said, and wet the end of the paper so it wouldn't stick to his lips.

He struck the match, inhaled deeply, blew a large white cloud out between us and thought for a long time about the piece of tobacco that was now on the tip of his tongue. His expression made him look like he was considering something he'd like to say to an old friend, then he spit the tobacco on the ground between us.

"I could help pay," I said. "I could get a job. Like you had to do for your family when you were thirteen."

Dad turned his head slightly, not quite looking at me, like maybe he was talking to the reserve over my shoulder.

"You think you're better than me because you were in the war," Dad said. "That's what makes you so smart? Well, I'd'a gone if I didn't have kids that needed feeding."

"It was just a dream, Dad."

Dad faced me full on.

"I sat with you for over two days. You said things in that fever I'd never heard spoke by a man who'd just breathed in too much Indian smoke. I believe you were on that ridge."

He stood and, with his cigarette still hanging from the corner of his mouth, he lifted the tobacco pouch from his shirt pocket and removed a cigarette he had rolled earlier.

"Take it."

I did as he said.

The cigarette trembled between my lips as Dad struck fire into the match head with a flick of his thumbnail. I hoped the breeze would kill the flame, but Dad cupped his rough hands as he raised the match.

I drew the heat and smoke into my lungs. In that second, my head felt as light and as easy as I could remember. When I lowered the cigarette, Dad put his arm across my shoulders.

"Let's go home," he said.

Later that night, when I was supposed to be long asleep, I heard Dad tell Mom that he'd lied to her, that her son had been on Vimy Ridge, that the wound in my shoulder had been caused by a blast so great that a German officer's coat button had been buried in her son's shoulder, that he was sorry there was something else in this world, something Indian that made the reverend's words and threats seem like nothing at all, that maybe the white God is not so strong after all.

Words came and went between them as my eyes grew heavy. For a while, I thought I heard Mom crying, then I realized it was Dad's voice, and I heard her say, "It's all the same God."

What a Terrible
Way to Go

I woke to the most horrible singing I had heard in my life.

It was Arthur.

I was afraid he'd found some of that army rum he'd been drinking on Vimy Ridge. I pulled on my pants and headed out to the kitchen, where Mom was sitting at the table drinking tea with cream and sugar.

"How long has he been here?"

"We had a whole pot of tea, waiting for you to wake up."

I headed outside, barefoot and shirtless. Arthur stood in the middle of the lane with the tire tracks on either side. He had his back to me, and he was peeing toward the road to Old Man Howe's farm.

I waited until he finished. I didn't need a fellow full of tea to turn too quickly, especially when Arthur could pee nearly ten feet.

"Hey, Stands Like Horse," I said, "you trying to make a river?"

Arthur grinned. "Hey, Friend Of Stands Like Horse,"

he said, giving everything a shake, stuffing it back into his pants and zipping up.

"We should build a dam before somebody gets drowned," I said.

"Get some shovels and we'll make a canal all the way to the gopher colony in Old Man Howe's cow pasture. We'll drown them out."

"What a terrible way to go."

"You boys want some more tea?" Mom called from inside. "I just put on a fresh pot!"

"No thanks, Mom!" I called back.

A few seconds later, the door squeaked open, and Mom walked quickly down the stairs toward the outhouse. She was nearly running when she pushed open the plywood door.

While Mom was busy, Arthur and I went back inside. I headed to my bedroom and finished dressing. When I came out, Arthur was drinking a cup of tea and Mom was pouring one for herself.

"Okay," I said, "but just one."

A half hour later, Mom was back in the outhouse, and Arthur and I were standing in our lane doing our best to flood out the gophers. We were all finished when Mom walked up behind us.

"I never saw much sense in it," she said, looking down at the river. "Men take an interest in things that are very odd to women."

She gave our shoulders a light pat.

"You're not taking Will today," Mom said. "And I

won't be hearing any argument from either of you."

"How'd you know?" Arthur asked.

"You're always planning something."

She headed back into the house.

"So what's the plan?" I asked.

"I don't know. Maybe we should ask your mom."

I elbowed Arthur in the ribs. Instead of giving me one back, he just got a look in his eyes I'd seen a hundred times before. Mom was right. Arthur had a plan.

A Foolish Thing to Do

Arthur headed up the lane like somebody who'd just got told he wasn't welcome.

"What's wrong?" I called.

"Nothing."

"Why're you leaving then?"

"Got important business."

"Where're you going?"

"To get Catface."

"What about the plan?"

"It includes Catface. I'll get him and bring him back here."

I caught up to Arthur as he turned south toward the reserve. Mom must have seen me pass the kitchen window because in a few seconds she was out the door, down the stairs and standing at the far end of our lane, where Dad usually parked the pickup.

I gave her a wave that meant I wasn't going anywhere.

"Get Catface? That's five miles there and five miles back. You'll be gone for the biggest part of three hours."

"With all that sugar?" Arthur said. "Heck, I'll be back before I leave."

"Well, don't go swimming the Atlantic. He's just down the railway tracks."

"The Pacific is closer?" He grinned, and headed toward the reserve.

"Say hello to General de Gaulle."

Mom had a confused look on her face.

"Arthur can go see anybody he wants to," Mom said. "But I don't want you sneaking off, even to talk to a general."

"It was just a joke, Mom. General de Gaulle's in France. I don't think I'd sneak all the way over there."

"You've been sneaking a lot worse places, from what Dad says."

"It was just a crazy dream," I said. "It seemed real at the time. But I can't see how something like that could really happen."

"Well, you've got Dad convinced," Mom said, her face turning red. "And I don't want you smoking."

"But Dad gave it to me."

"And his dad got him started. It was a foolish thing to do then, and it's still a foolish thing to do."

"It wasn't so bad," I said. "Heck, I never even coughed."

Before I could get my hand up, she'd slapped me across the ear. It wasn't a hard slap. Heck, I'd hit myself harder pretending to make myself wake up. It's just that hitting was Dad's job. She hadn't hit me for any reason for as long as I could remember, and I didn't like the way it made me feel inside.

She put her arms around my neck and pulled me to her. I could feel her tears falling in my hair and down my neck. They felt warm.

"I know I've caused trouble for you and Dad," I said. "I don't mean to."

Mom's body started to shake, but not a sound came from her. The quiet crying was the worst kind. It made me think about Mom dying. Pretty soon I was crying, too.

"I'm so scared," she finally said. "I dream sometimes right in broad daylight —" She bit her lip to keep from crying more. "I see the Mountie coming up our lane. I want to run, but I'm frozen right in this spot. I know he's come to tell me he's found you in a ditch. That you're dead. I want to hit him. I want to make him hurt for hurting me. But he never comes closer than standing behind his car door."

"I'd never do that to you, Mom."

"You can't stop it. I just pray I go first."

I put all my will into holding back my tears, but I couldn't even slow one drop. If, at thirteen, I couldn't manage that, I didn't know how I'd stop Mom's dream from coming true.

The Road to Blackening His Heart

I was lying in a trampled area of tall grass between our house and the field to the east, trying not to fall asleep again, when I heard a low snorting sound.

For a second, it seemed as if somebody had called my name. Where Dad usually parked our pickup were two horses. Behind them, on a flat-topped wagon, sat Arthur and Catface, and behind them, Emma lay on a layer of straw bales. Under her head was loose straw arranged for a pillow. She looked asleep.

Behind them all, Dad's pickup rolled to a stop.

Seeing Catface reminded me I still had Old Man Howe's forty dollars in my hip pocket, money I had taken to run Catface off his and Emma's land. Emma made me think of the money even more. If anybody deserved Howe's money, it was his daughter Emma. Then I thought of the four hundred and fifty dollars Dad owed the hospital for saving my life, and the whole thing started to make sense. Old Man Howe was putting just enough money in a poor person's hand to turn him down the road to blackening his heart.

I looked up as the pickup's engine chugged to a stop.

I expected Dad to start hollering and cussing like he usually did when somebody did the opposite of what he had told them to do. The pickup's door opened and Dad stepped out, lifted his hat and scratched his head. He looked more confused than mad. Before Dad could push the door closed, Mom was down the front steps.

"Would you look at this, Dad?" she said. "Looks like we've got company for dinner."

"Looks more like a thrashing crew to me," Dad said.

Mom moved past the horses, touched Catface gently on the knee and stopped at the rear of the wagon, where Emma was asleep in the straw.

"We're there, Grandma," Catface said, leaned back and poked her on shoulder. "Time to wake up."

She sat with a jerk and stared right at Mom, her eyes as big around as tea cups.

"*Suietapi.*"

Mom turned to Catface and shrugged.

"Water-person," he said. "Grandma's roof's been leaking since the thunderstorm. She's started calling herself *Suietapi.*"

Emma pulled down on Catface's ear.

"Ouch."

"Do not go talking about this family's business," she said, now fully awake. "We do not need these good people thinking we can't manage our affairs. Or that we are in need of something we can't afford."

That said, she swung off the wagon and stood in front of Mom. When Mom did nothing except open her mouth and let out a slow breath, Emma took Mom's hand and shook it hard.

"My name is Emma Howe," she said. "Catface is my grandson. You all know my father, Clarence Howe. You do not have to say anything about him. I know he is not well liked by certain people. And, truthfully, I am still searching my own heart for some tenderness for the man."

She gave Mom's hand a hard pump, dropped it and walked up to Dad.

Dad stuck out his hand, then realized he was still holding his hat.

"I understand you have a partial roll of roofing paper," she said.

I'd forgotten all about her leaky roof. She didn't give me a look. She didn't have to. I felt as if every word had been directed at me.

"I —" Dad paused and closed his hand tightly around the hat — "maybe. I haven't looked for a while. I suppose. Why?"

"Roofing paper!" Mom said in a loud voice. "What we need is tea and biscuits. Let's go inside where we can all sit and talk in comfort."

Mom's answer to the troubles in this life was tea, soda biscuits and sitting at the table.

"I just put on a fresh pot," Mom said, and headed inside.

Emma followed Mom.

Dad was close behind, still trying to figure out what to do with his hat.

She's Sick of Gettin' Rained On

Catface unhitched the horses and followed as they wandered off toward the irrigation ditch, like they could smell the water.

"Why'd you bring Emma?" I asked Arthur.

"I didn't. She brought me."

"I don't understand what she wants here. Did she hear you talking to Catface about your plan?"

"I didn't have time to talk to anybody," Arthur said. "I got a mile out and there comes Catface driving Watcher's team and wagon. I jumped on, and here I am. Were you asleep or something?"

Of course I was, but admitting it would just get me an elbow in the ribs.

"What's she want with Mom and Dad?" I asked. "Is she going to get us in trouble over this Wilfred Black stuff?"

"You're already in as much trouble as is possible for somebody she likes," Arthur said. "Remember that roof you said you'd fix?"

"I guess I forgot about that."

"Well, she didn't. Now she's come to get somebody to fix it right."

"Dad?"

Arthur shook his head. "She's come to talk to your dad about the way you keep your word."

"I was in the hospital."

"She said you could'a sent her a message."

"How? Smoke signals?"

"She's not very happy," Catface said when he got back from checking that the horses didn't get hit by a truck when they crossed the road to the irrigation ditch. "She's sick of gettin' rained on."

"You two could'a fixed it."

"Arthur was too busy with his friend. I haven't seen him 'til an hour ago."

"Arthur, you didn't have to wait around the hospital for two days waiting to see if I'd die."

Arthur gave me an elbow in the ribs.

From inside the house came a big roar — three voices all laughing together.

"Besides," Catface said, "Grandma doesn't trust us, especially when she figures we're up to something. She wants to keep us together so she can watch us."

"Does she know about the sweat lodge?"

"Not yet," Arthur said, glancing over his shoulder at the house and the sound of dying laughter. "But I expect she'll find out pretty soon. If I know Emma Howe at all, she won't leave 'til she's satisfied your mom and dad have told her everything about everything."

"Arthur told you?" I asked Catface.

"On the way here. After Grandma fell asleep."

Arthur was staring at me with the same look he'd had when he'd shot Pots. I knew he hadn't told that part of the story.

"You gotta tell him, Arthur. Heck, Emma's probably hearing it right now."

"Why? Nothing's changed. He's still here. He's still mean and ugly."

"And alive."

"Okay, I shot him. Are you happy now?"

"Yeah," I said.

But Arthur didn't stop. He got mad. "I shot him a hundred times!"

"Who?" Catface asked.

"Pots!" Arthur hollered. "But it didn't matter. Nothing's changed."

"You must've missed him," Catface said.

"I shot him here and here and here," Arthur said, poking Catface hard all over the chest. "I didn't miss."

"Okay!" Catface pushed Arthur's hand away. "Will nearly died from a shoulder wound, and Pots came home without a scratch. I don't understand."

"I don't either," Arthur said.

"Come on, Arthur," I said. "Most of those hundred shots hit the dirt. I figured you had it in for German trenches you shot them up so bad. If you hit Pots once, you were darn lucky."

"Why don't you just shut up, Will?" Arthur said.

Before we could say another word, the door squeaked open and Mom came walking down the stairs. Emma and Dad followed her. Dad still had his hat in his hand.

"Boys," Emma called, "you've got some work to do."

Catface ran to get the horses. Arthur seemed to have gone back to the dark place he'd been in when he thought he'd killed Pots. I had a feeling Arthur was asking the same thing I was — how could my wound be real and Pots's wounds not be? Either Arthur and I never really left the sweat lodge, or Pots was wounded but didn't die.

I hadn't heard Arthur's plan, but I could see only one thing to do: I'd have to find out if Pots had been wounded. I'd have to see the scars to say for sure that he'd killed Wilfred. Without them, I couldn't say if Vimy Ridge had just been a dream caused by Indian smoke, if Wilfred had been killed in action like the government papers said or if he'd died by accident like the letter to his mother had said.

German Officer

The horses pulled back against Catface's lead and had the look that said they weren't done eating, drinking or relaxing. I was afraid I was going to find out I felt just as they did in another few hours, when we got back to Emma's leaky-roofed shack in the woods.

As Catface hitched the horses to the wagon, Dad and Arthur tossed all but one straw bale off its deck.

"Move that one up front where I can listen to these three boys," Emma said.

Dad set the last bale right behind the driver.

Emma nodded.

I stood off to the side near where Mom was considering the ongoing work. I rubbed my shoulder and pretended to try and stretch out the muscles, then made a painful expression and let my arm drop limp to my side. When all I got were smirks and eyes rolled back, I said to nobody, "I'll get that roll of roofing paper."

"And I'll get some biscuits and tea for your trip back to Emma's place," Mom said, and headed inside. A few seconds later, she was singing a song about bringing in the sheaves.

I hoped I wasn't going to have to help with harvest.

Dad made a low grumbling sound that meant he was getting ready to cuss somebody good.

"Damnation, what are you doing with that horse?" he asked Catface. "When's the last time you hitched a team?"

"This morning?"

"And this is what you call hitched? Who taught you?"

"Nobody. I learned myself."

"Well, no damned wonder these horses don't want to work for you. You got them workin' against the wagon and each other."

"They did okay so far."

"Watch your mouth, boy."

Emma took Catface by the earlobe and pushed him away from the horses.

"Hey!" he complained.

"I have made a business arrangement with Mr. Samson," she said, and let go of his ear. "If he says you did it wrong, you watch him and get it right for next time."

Catface kicked the dirt and stepped back. He didn't turn away, but I knew it wasn't Dad that had him paying attention. It was his grandma's warnings.

When Dad finished hitching the horses, he used his hat to knock the straw from the deck. He got up and sat with his feet on the hitch and his forearms on his knees. He moved the reins easy across the horses' backs and made a clicking sound out the side of his mouth. The team pulled past us and stopped.

"They're not going to let us out of their sight," Catface finally said. "They've been making a plan of their own."

"They can't watch us every second," Arthur said.

"Grandma doesn't have to. She'll shame us into it."

"She can't shame Will." Arthur put his arm over my shoulder.

"Yes, she can."

Arthur let his hand cup the wound, still covered with the bandage.

"We've got something they won't expect," Arthur said. "The bit of German officer inside Will."

I pushed Arthur's hand from my shoulder. "Is that your big plan? You're going to blow me up in front of Pots and hope one of my buttons kills him dead?"

"Shush, Will. I don't have a plan. I just figured if I let on I had one you'd go all crazy trying to make one even better. Like you always do."

"I don't always do that."

"Maybe not always. But, for sure, ever since we were six."

"That's when we met. That makes it always."

"Okay," Arthur said, "how about if we work out a plan together? All three of us."

"I'm not going back into that sweat lodge, Arthur. I'm not going to that darn ridge. And I'm not going to kill Pots."

"What if I got a town girl to give you a chicken feather right on Main Street?"

"I'm not a coward. And it's a white feather that means a man's a coward, not some stupid chicken feather."

"Boys," Emma called. "The work is over here."

"You're crazy, Arthur," I said.

"You're welcome to all the shiplap you can carry," Dad said. "I got plenty of tar paper too. And there's the shingles I told you about."

Dad was talking and pointing here and there at different piles of wood.

"But I'm short on heavy timbers," he continued. "I wouldn't trust those poplar branches the boys trimmed either. You'll have to pick up some four-by-fours in town."

"What do you mean I'm welcome to it?" Emma asked. "I intend to pay you the going rate for used wood. I'm not looking for charity. I've already agreed I'd pay you after harvest."

Dad took off his hat and rung it like a dish rag.

"Dammit, woman!" Dad said. "You don't need to take offense at every word I say. I meant you're welcome to it at the going price."

"That's better," Emma said.

A few seconds later, Catface and Arthur were busy stacking shiplap.

Dad stood back watching his piles of lumber disappear down to nothing, lumber he'd scrounged for three years to build a workshop. He turned and walked his hard, steady pace back to the house.

There wasn't enough lumber to cover my hospital bill, but it was a pretty big chunk, maybe even two hundred dollars' worth.

Dad was a pretty good scrounger.

I thought about Old Man Howe's forty dollars. If I gave it to Dad, I'd have to run off my friend, or I'd be a liar and a cheat, just like Old Man Howe wanted me to be. I hated that money.

Old Wounds

I sat with my good shoulder touching Catface as he drove the team to town. Arthur sat on the other side of Catface. Emma sat on the straw bale behind us, ready to smack us or pull an ear if we started whispering.

I could see the whole thing clearer now that I was quiet and the wagon was rocking gently and the horses were clopping easy down the gravel road. Mom didn't want me getting killed in a ditch or in a trench real or made real by Indian smoke. Emma didn't want us — especially her grandson — getting into trouble trying to set history right. And Dad was in no mood for another four-hundred-dollar hospital bill, where maybe he'd have to tear the wood off his own house to pay for my life. It would be tough for me and Arthur and Catface to even pee in the woods without somebody knowing about it.

Town was a little over a mile west of my house, so it took hardly any time to get there, but still the silent ride gave me plenty of thinking room. I leaned forward only once to take a look at Arthur, to see if he was looking at me, or if he had the look of a plan in his eyes. When I heard the straw bale move under

Emma's weight, as if she'd leaned toward me, I put my hand over my ear and stared down at the road and the bits of gravel and dust lifting from the horses' hooves.

My thoughts kept coming back to Pots. I knew I'd have a good chance of being sent to hell by Mom's reverend, but a small, mean part of me wished that Pots had died on Vimy Ridge, that Arthur really had shot him dead. Then this would all be over, and I wouldn't be tormented by what I knew I had to do. I knew there were men in Grayson, maybe even Arthur and Catface or my own dad, who could take a gun and finish this business in a hurry. I was afraid that was the plan Arthur had said he really didn't have. I knew I couldn't do that, not even to Pots. But I was afraid I might have to hurt a friend to save Pots from a bullet.

Catface turned the team left at the United Church and eased up, letting the horses use the gentle downward slope of Main Street and the weight of the wagonload of lumber to choose their own pace.

A man came out of Frankie's store, then stopped and watched us roll toward him. His legs looked too long for his body. His hair was white and his ears stuck out like he'd cupped them forward, trying to hear our thoughts.

Pots.

I tried to remember the Blackfoot word that Arthur had called him, the one that meant "weasel in winter coat," but all I could remember was *Akaiiniu* — "he is dead." I whispered this to myself and felt Emma's hand move to my ear, then pat my neck instead.

I could see Arthur sitting straight and tall, his muscles tight as he stared at Pots, like he was looking at something horrible that brought out the thousand years of warrior blood pumping through his body.

When we approached Grierson Street, Emma Howe leaned forward with her face between me and her grandson.

"Turn right," she said, "and don't look at him."

Maybe Catface could look away, but I couldn't. I kept wondering what was under Pots's shirt, long-sleeved and buttoned all the way to his neck. But he had his eyes fixed on Arthur, with an expression that first seemed to only hold confusion, then shifted to pain as he moved his hand over his chest, slowly, as if touching old wounds. I found my own hand move to my wounded shoulder and press down as if to stop my blood.

Catface snapped the reins across the horses' backs, and with the slope and the short rest, they jerked hard and strong on the hitch and lurched forward.

Emma's feet struck me in the head when she fell backward onto the wagon deck in the space between her straw bale and the stack of shiplap.

Wood banged and clattered as she tried to stand.

Pots turned, ran up the street and disappeared behind the wood covering his broken window.

"Whoa!" Catface hollered, and leaned back against the reins.

Muscles rippled across the horses' backs. Dust and gravel rolled out from under their hooves. The wagon jerked and the horses let out a loud snort.

Emma tumbled forward and landed with her arms draped over Catface's shoulders. Her eyes were big and round. The bun that held her hair neatly in place had come undone, and long graying strands hung across her face.

We sat her up as Pots came back out of his office carrying the short baseball bat he kept behind his office chair.

"It's you," he said to Arthur, and swung the bat.

Arthur was already falling back onto the wagon deck and the bat caught Catface's baggy shirt sleeve. The speed of the head tore the cotton like it had been hooked with a claw hammer. The bat just missed Arthur's chest and the tip of his upturned chin, then came to a stop over Pots's left shoulder. His face was blue with rage as he swung the bat a few inches above the wooden deck.

"You no-good, red son of a —" Pots cussed over his bent arm.

But Arthur had rolled from the wagon and landed with a thump in the gravel and dust of Main Street. Catface dived between the horses.

The bat smacked the near horse on the right hip. In a second, Catface was lying on his back, the wagon's steel axle slicing through the air above his thin body.

By now I was sitting in the middle of the street, along with long lengths of shiplap and Emma.

Pots didn't see any of it. He'd swung at Arthur like a wild man, missing all three times.

Catface ran to his grandma. I stood in the middle

of Main Street, halfway between Arthur and Emma. Pots had stopped cussing. He was breathing hard and heavy as he swung the bat like a beaten boxer throwing his last few punches.

I timed my move with his swing — running hard and low, like I was under artillery fire. Pots hit me with the back of his hand, a soft blow across my mouth that caught me by surprise and had me tasting blood. When he turned to Arthur, I grabbed his shirt and jerked his collar toward me. His narrow shoulders pulled back and his arm dropped weakly to his side. A button popped and landed at Arthur's feet. I put everything I had into one last pull.

I landed in the gravel with the shirt in my hands. It was damp with new sweat.

Pots cussed, the bat dragging at his feet as he turned from Arthur to me, his bleached white skin bright in the August sun, the four scars paler still where the machine-gun bullets had tore at his shoulder and the heavy muscle at the base of his neck. The last and worst wound was just above his right breast. When he turned, I saw the bullet had gone clean through.

A short distance up the street, Emma was standing with Catface, staring at Pots's bare chest. Big silent tears rolling down her cheeks, as if all her hopes had been uncovered and now were lost.

I dropped Pots's shirt and rubbed my hands on my pant legs. All around me, the air stunk of mud, dead rats and human waste.

None of That Matters Anymore

Dad's old pickup turned left at the United Church and headed toward us. The closer he got the slower he drove and the more he hunched over his steering wheel. When he got to the first piece of shiplap lying in the gravel, the engine jerked and stalled. Dad looked out his side window at me and Arthur and Catface and Emma, then slowly turned and stared out the other side, as if he expected to see a tornado heading away from the mess all over Main Street. There was nothing there but the space between the butcher shop and the library that once held the old Grayson Café, the one Dad tore down to make our house.

He eased the pickup door open and stood with his hat in his hand.

It was not yet one o'clock and most businesses were still closed for dinner.

"What in darnation?" he said, and blinked at Catface. "Did I hitch the rig wrong?"

Pots was long gone, but his shirt was lying in a crumpled pile in the gravel. Dad turned and stared at it, then he glanced at us as if to check if we were all fully dressed.

Emma gave us each a slap on whatever she could reach without moving too far. I got one on the rear, Catface on the shoulder and Arthur on the top of his head.

My heart felt good. I didn't like seeing her crying when she saw the wounds on Pots's chest, the way it brought back all those hard years she'd spent in the woods hidden by her own father, waiting and hoping for her husband to return from Vimy Ridge, and all the while the lie was walking the streets of Grayson in the form of a coward.

"Fetch the wagon." She gave Catface an extra swat. "And reload my lumber."

She put her hand over her knee and tried to walk toward Dad. In a second, he was at her side, helping her to the truck.

"Is Mrs. Samson any good at bruises and scrapes?" she asked.

"She's fair," Dad said. "You sure you don't want a doctor?"

"I'll let your wife decide."

She held Dad's arm as he eased the passenger door open.

"Mr. Samson and I will be doing some business at the lumber yard," she said. "If he doesn't mind the detour."

Dad nodded.

"When you boys get the wagon loaded," she added, "stop by and pick up the four-by-fours we'll have ordered. If nothing else, I'll have a roof over my head."

Dad helped her into the pickup.

"You sure you want to leave them alone?" Dad asked. "They're bound to get into trouble."

"None of that matters anymore," she said. "I believe the boys really were on Vimy Ridge. I believe all of it now."

"Believing doesn't change nothing," Dad said, and tossed his hat onto his side of the seat. "I can't help you if it's going to make trouble for my family. I ain't going to do that. Your troubles with Pots or your dad is your business."

"I'm not asking for your help," she said. "I just want you to stay out of my way."

"What can you do? Your dad had you locked in that shack for nearly thirty years because you married Wilfred Black. You want him to do it again because you figure he sent Pots to kill Black?"

She slammed the door closed and rolled the window down.

"Are you going to take me to Mrs. Samson or not?"

He stomped around to his door and glared over the truck box at me and Arthur and Catface. "What are you three gawking at?" he said. "You need more work?"

Dad sat beside Emma and stared out the windshield. "Tell me what you want done," he said.

"Say the truth."

"To who?"

"Everybody."

"The whole damned town?"

"Yes."

"What are you going to do?"

"The same as you."

"And you figure that'll do some good?"

If she answered, I didn't hear.

One Fight in a Day
Is Enough

Me and Arthur and Catface followed the trail of lumber up Main Street, turned right past the hardware store, where the horses had dumped Emma out onto the gravel, and headed on up the alley, working our way west behind the beer parlor. Along the way, we made small stacks of about six boards each and set them to the side, where nobody would drive over them and wreck them for everything but firewood.

Joe Warren, the one-armed man from Vimy Ridge, came out of his second-floor room above the beer parlor and stopped on the landing. Though I'd heard of him for most of my life, I'd really only seen him since Arthur and I got into all that trouble during the last week of school, when we found Yellowfly left for dead near the railway tracks. After the whole town blamed the train for Yellowfly's injuries, Arthur and I followed a string of clues that led to the real criminals: Woody Loewan, Pots and Joe Warren. Back then, I called Warren Singing Man because he sang the dirty "Three German Soldiers" song when he was drunk.

That was most of the time. Normally he cussed me anytime he saw me, hollering mean things about Indians, but now he said nothing, though he was pretty drunk.

He stared at Arthur with a look I'd seen before, thirty-five years ago, when Wilfred and Arthur removed his dead arm to save his life.

Arthur's muscles tightened, and he seemed to grow taller.

"Come on, Arthur. One fight in a day is enough."

I thought Warren would attack us like Pots had done. But he just stared at Arthur as he took one slow step at a time down the wooden stairs.

As he got closer, I could smell the cigarette smoke and beer on him. I wanted to turn away and take a clean breath. Beside me, Catface let the lumber drop with a clatter. Nobody moved but Warren, inching his way toward us. Catface clenched his fists and spread his feet to steady himself if a blow came. Arthur's breathing became short and shallow.

"Don't come any closer," I said with a shaky voice. "We don't want to have to hurt you."

He moved toward Arthur as if I didn't exist, as if Catface didn't exist, as if nothing in the world existed except him and Arthur.

His red, drunken eyes moved across Arthur's face. The stump under the loose shirt sleeve twitched like it remembered, too. Warren moved his hand up the sleeve and steadied the remains of his arm.

His rheumy eyes searched Arthur's. For a few long seconds, I thought I saw a spark of recognition. Then it was gone, and he bowed his head until his chin touched his chest.

"You dropped your lumber," he finally said.

"We had a runaway wagon," Arthur answered.

"I heard 'em." He glanced over his shoulder. "They headed that way."

"Thanks," Arthur said. "We'll be following them now."

Catface and I restacked the boards and slid them out from between Warren and Arthur, then moved on, working our way from piece to piece to the end of the alley.

When Catface and I turned back, neither Warren nor Arthur had moved. Then Arthur took the loose shirt sleeve and turned it up in folds that matched the width of the cuff. At the base of Warren's stump, Arthur took a safety pin he used to hold his shirt closed where some buttons were missing and pinned Warren's sleeve so it stayed neat. All the while, Warren watched Arthur with that same trusting, confused look. Then this man full of hate, who'd tried once to kill an Indian, took Arthur's hand and shook it like a friend.

He'd Seen a Friend Inside Him

We followed the trail of strewn lumber, stacking it as we went, all the way to Arthur's place. The team and wagon stood in the shade cast by the house. Watcher, who owned the team, was carrying a bucket of water from the iron pump. Arthur's grandpa sat on the railway tie that made the front step. Beside him was a tin cup full of tea with a piece of bannock set across the top so the steam would soften it to where Grandpa could eat without chewing his teeth down to the gums. Bannock always tasted good, but it could get pretty tough.

Watcher set the bucket on the ground between the horses and rubbed his hand down his favorite horse's mane.

"Who hitched this team?" he asked.

I gave Catface a chance to answer. When it looked like we'd probably stand there forever, I answered for him.

"My dad did."

Watcher ran his fingertips up the collar and then

under the hame tugs.

"Good job," he said. "But if he'd hitched them the Indian way, they'd've only run a short distance. Most of your lumber would still be on the wagon and there'd be no need for all this picking up."

I felt my face flush with embarrassment.

Catface gave me an easy elbow in the ribs.

That just made me feel worse.

Watcher patted the horse again and grinned.

"I'm going to have to remember how your dad did this," he finally said.

"*Iikitamapiu*," Grandpa said to me. "'It is very amusing.' Big Indian joke. Seventy-five years of reserve and Indians still making jokes."

"Come on," Catface said, "we better get the lumber loaded and hauled to Grandma's." Then Catface turned to Watcher. "When do you need your wagon back?"

Watcher shrugged and made a shooing sign for us to go. "I'm gettin' used to walkin'."

Catface turned the team around, Arthur and I climbed on, and we headed out to our piles of shiplap all the way back to Main Street.

Once we got to the alley behind the beer parlor, I saw that someone had moved the stack of boards Catface and I had piled while Joe Warren and Arthur stood facing each other. When Arthur and I bent to lift the boards onto the wagon, the back door to the beer parlor opened about quarter way and Warren's face appeared. He seemed to be almost sober, a sight I had never seen before.

Again, Arthur stared back at him, holding the stack of lumber. It took a long time before Warren eased the door closed, then Arthur turned to me.

"We don't have all day," he said, and heaved his end of the stack onto the wagon.

Catface drove on, all of us staring straight ahead like we were waiting for someone to say something we didn't have to think about, like pike fishing, or duck hunting. But in all that silence was a lot of thinking. Here was Joe Warren, who'd lived a life of hatred, who'd blinded an Indian man in one eye, but was now searching Arthur's eyes like he'd seen a friend inside him. And here was Arthur, who had wished Joe Warren to hell, but had just pinned his sleeve and taken his hand like the day he rescued me from the gang of Indian boys and left his touch on me like we'd been friends forever.

We passed Mr. Phillips and my dad fitting a new piece of plate glass into Pots's office. Along the back wall of the office was a line of pockmarks like a spray of machine-gun fire, but it was probably just rocks spun up from under a pickup's tire as somebody raced away.

Pots was nowhere in sight, but I could feel the hitch push up against my feet as Arthur's muscles tightened.

"Are the four-by-fours ready to pick up?" I called to Dad.

"They've been waiting for over two hours," he said. "Where'd you find the wagon? Calgary?"

"At Arthur's house."

"What took you so long?"

"There was shiplap all the way there," I said. "Some was even in the ditch."

Mr. Phillips grinned, like Dad had been bragging about how best to hitch a team so it wouldn't get too tired.

"When do you want me home?" I asked.

"When you do the job you promised Emma Howe you'd do last Sunday."

My face got hot.

Catface gave me a gentle elbow in the ribs, and the weight of the hitch eased under my feet.

While we were loading the four-by-fours, I started talking about a time at Horse Shoe Backwater when I hooked a pike so big it nearly dragged me clear across to the other side, broke my fishing line and then left me there for two weeks because I was still too young to know how to swim. Dad finally found me after Mom said I hadn't been eating my suppers. He figured I was probably still fishing, so he went to the backwater and saw me nearly starved to death. He tossed his lure and hooked me by the pant leg and reeled me back. Afterward, he said it was a good thing I'd lost so much weight or he wouldn't have been able to rescue me, and he'd have had to let me skinny down to bones before he could pull me back to his side.

Arthur and Catface were staring at me.

"What?" I said.

"You let a pike that big get away?" Arthur said.

As we headed back to Emma's shack, we laughed and joked and told stories, mostly made-up ones, some true but stretched until the truthful parts were awfully thin, and others that were just a string of lies. It felt good to only think of *Iikitamapiu*, "it is very amusing," Indian jokes still all around me even after seventy-five years of reserves.

Why Chase the Past?

We headed east out of town with our restacked shiplap, new four-by-four timbers set on top, and the whole lot tied down with a triple layer of binder twine from the lumber yard. All the way down the two miles of gravel to the main highway, Arthur talked about a time when his grandpa rode with Lame Bull and his Blackfeet raiders from Montana. There wasn't a horse or a female that was safe, Arthur claimed.

I decided to ignore the rest of their conversation, which was hard to do considering they were cussing so much. Cussing was the part of Blackfoot I understood the best.

Once we got to the highway and the wagon took on an easy side-to-side motion, I thought we would fall asleep sitting up. Then a big truck would come roaring up from behind and our eyes would pop open like Emma had just slapped us on the back of our heads. But in less than a minute, our heads would be bobbing again until the next truck passed.

My stomach was grumbling about supper when Catface reined in on the team at the start of the trail heading to Emma's shack and its leaky roof.

I got off the wagon and opened the barbed wire gate. That reminded me of Old Man Howe and the curse his forty dollars held over me.

As Catface eased the team between the pair of split cedar fence posts, he seemed to sit taller and straighter, the way he always looked on that piece of white man's land now owned by him and Emma, that little bump on the straight line the railway made as the border of the reserve.

I dragged the post and wire back and hooked the gate closed, climbed on the wagon and sat beside Arthur. The trail was well worn now, not like almost two months ago, when Catface was on the run from Old Man Howe and Emma was a prisoner in the shack. The wagon ruts squeezed through the perimeter of thin young trees, twisted and turned among the tall old poplars and finally eased past the small clearing where Arthur's grandpa and I had turned back Old Man Howe and his men, then on up alongside the pile of broken branches we'd stacked the morning after the big thunderstorm.

Fifty feet ahead, just in front of the shack, Emma sat on straw bales arranged like a sofa chair. Above her, tied among the trees, was the tarp we'd slept under during the storm. She had a bandage on one knee, another on her elbow and two pieces of gauze held to her cheek with strips of white tape.

As she tried to stand, she looked awfully stiff and sore. When she got to halfway, she slowly settled back down into her straw chair.

"Help me up!" she called.

We tripped over one another getting off the wagon, putting our hands under her arms and trying to lift her to her feet.

"Good Lord," she said, and slapped Arthur's hand down. "I only want to stand. I don't want to get thrown over my own roof."

Catface and I got her to standing and held her steady in case she decided to move. I could smell the strong Watkins ointment Mom put on cuts and scrapes.

"Let go of me," she said, pushing our hands away like they were dirty. "I'm just stiff from sitting and waiting for you three to get back. Now get up on that roof before I take a broom to you."

We tripped over one another again, trying to get up on the roof.

"What's wrong with your grandma?" Arthur asked.

Before Catface could answer, Emma called, "Nothing three hours of sawing and hammering won't fix!"

That ended any talk that didn't have something directly to do with fixing and repairing.

The roof was the shape of a lean-to — sloping in only one direction. The very outside layer was long straight poplars like tepee poles, set every foot or so, holding down about a hundred layers of tar paper. Below that was a layer of half-rotten shiplap, and under that were the sagging poplar logs the new four-by-fours were to replace. Tearing something apart was easy, putting it all back together so it worked could be a lot tougher.

Grandma was wrong about the sawing and hammering taking three hours. It took all the way until dark and we still weren't finished, and probably wouldn't be for a good part of the next day, but the worst — the heavy lifting and the thinking — was done. If it rained, though, she'd be even wetter than before.

All through our working, when I wasn't straightening old nails and spikes or trying not to saw a finger off or pound my thumb into the shiplap, I watched Emma. She never sat down, even once, until we all did. She didn't move very fast, but she didn't stop either. If I'd been that sore, I would've been lying down crying.

It was past sunset when we gave up on getting done that day. Me and Arthur and Catface washed in a bucket of well water that Emma had left warming in the afternoon sun. The soap and the cloth felt so good on my skin that I let out a happy little moan.

Afterward, we sat around the fire she'd built because she didn't want to cook inside and risk smoking us off the shack and maybe never getting her roof repaired. She dished up supper from a big cast iron frying pan heaping with dried deer meat cooked in bacon fat and onions with boiled potatoes cut into slices and fried until they were golden brown and piled on a plate so big I let out another moan of joy. We ate until the pan was empty, then we sopped up the bacon and deer and onion juice with the soda biscuits Mom had sent.

When we were done burping and picking our teeth and the tea was all drank and the whole world had suddenly become a perfect place and all my thoughts of Pots and Joe Warren and Vimy Ridge were gone maybe forever, Emma asked, "What now?"

"I expect we'll get the roof waterproofed before noon," I answered.

Emma put her hard old hand on my knee and squeezed gently.

"I saw the bullet wounds on that man's chest," she said. "I know the truth when I see it."

It seemed to me that she'd waited until none of us had the strength to resist, or lie, or just look at our feet and pretend everything was okay.

"I think I can get Joe Warren to help us," Arthur said. "But after being drunk for thirty-five years, I don't know what he remembers."

For the first time since I met Catface, he didn't have anything to say when the talk turned to his grandpa, and I was just trying to put the image of the sweat lodge out of my mind.

"Don't worry about my father," Emma said. "What we can't do to him on this earth, others will do to him. I believe his time here is ending."

"So why chase the past when we can't change nothing?" I asked.

She moved her eyes over our faces, the campfire leaving just a hint of red on her cheeks. I saw her now as the young woman she'd been in 1917, when she was only sixteen, the wife of an Indian man and mother of a half-breed baby her own father hated. In that moment, I wondered if the Indian medicine was at work under the great dome of night.

"I want to know the truth," she said. "That will be enough."

She put one hand on her grandson's shoulder and the other on Arthur's and pushed to get up. When I stood to help her, she shook her head. It seemed to take all the strength she had left in her body, but she finally stood. Before she headed back to her cabin and her bed in the corner of the dirt floor, she touched Catface on the top of the head.

"You stay with me," she said. "We'll finish the roof tomorrow."

"What about us?" I asked. "Dad said I should stay 'til this is done."

"You and Arthur have some snooping to do in town."

"What about Dad?"

"I'll manage the fathers."

"I want to go, too," Catface said. "The roof can wait for a few more days."

"I need you here," Emma said.

"If you make me stay, I won't do anything. I'll just sit in the sun all day long, like a lazy Indian."

"Don't get smart with me."

"What good is the truth, if nobody ever has to pay?"

"It will make a difference when the whole town knows."

"This town? They already know. They've known what your dad did to you for thirty-five years."

I was still rising when Emma made a quick step toward Catface, like she was going to slap some respect into him. She only got half a step when her knee buckled. She hit the ground hard and lurched forward, landing with her hands out in front of her.

Arthur caught Catface by the elbow. "You're staying here."

"Make me," Catface said.

Arthur hit Catface flat in the chest with a double blow from the heels of his hands.

Catface's air left his body in a sudden, silent puff. When he landed on his rear end, his face was turning blue and he sounded like a gassed soldier on Vimy Ridge.

"There's some whiskey under my mattress," Emma said to me. "Help me sit, then fetch it."

I did as she asked, trying not to look under the bed, where the sharpened broomstick might be hiding. Sliding my hand under her mattress, I caught the neck of the small flat mickey. I returned and handed it to her.

"It's not for me" — she paused like she was having second thoughts, then forced the words out — "you'll need it to convince Joe Warren to do what you need him to."

Half an hour later, Catface was inside the cabin helping his grandma, Arthur had hitched the team, and we were on our way back through the woods toward Grayson.

The night was moonless and black, the big trucks had all pulled over to rest their engines and let their drivers sleep, Arthur was as still as he'd been since we returned from Vimy Ridge, and I felt so alone I thought that maybe I understood the comfort men like Joe Warren found in the bottle, that maybe life would be okay if only I could never remember anything ever again.

Breathing for Two Men

It was well past midnight when we rolled to a stop behind the beer parlor. I couldn't tell by a watch, because I'd never owned one, or by the stars, because I was never as good at telling time by them as I was at using the sun. But I did know the beer parlor closed at midnight and the drunks usually wandered around for nearly an hour complaining about the beer they left half drunk, hollering and cussing as they looked for their cars or trucks. Everybody was gone. I figured if it was too late for them it was too late for me.

"Come on, Arthur. Let's go home."

Arthur just sat like he was still driving the team, the reins resting easy in his hands, his eyes moving to the narrow wooden stairs leading to Joe Warren's room.

On the landing, the door was ajar. The room was dark and silent.

"He's drunk," I said. "He can't tell us nothing tonight. Maybe not ever."

"I'm going up," Arthur said.

I did nothing but motion with my hand like maybe he'd forgotten where Warren lived, but it really meant he'd have to do it alone because I wasn't moving, not for the Queen of England, and certainly not for a hating, drunken old fool like Warren. I'd had more of him than I could stand when he tried to kick me in the face during the last week of school, when he thought I looked too much like an Indian for his liking.

Arthur set his foot on the first step like he was testing its strength. When he grabbed the two-by-four handrail, the rotten post it was nailed to came clear out of the ground. He set the rail down again and, with his back touching the building, inched his way up the stairs to the narrow landing.

I pushed the straw bale back with my elbows, leaned my head on its soft surface and closed my eyes. The door creaked open. When I figured he was inside, I opened my eyes, stared up at the night and all the stars God stuck on the great dome of his sweat lodge. I had just found Polaris when I heard the smack of a fist on bare skin, like somebody getting punched very hard.

"Will!" Arthur called.

Then again, *smack!*

I jumped off the wagon, crossed the gravel alley and grabbed the handrail. I swung my legs to the second step. Then the railing snapped from its post and swung up like it was following me. In a second, I had landed in the foxtail with a hard thump.

Smack!

I scrambled on my hands and knees up the stairs. In the flickering candlelight, I saw Arthur swinging his fist and Joe Warren lying on the linoleum floor.

Smack! The blow landed square in the middle of Warren's chest. His body twitched, then went still.

"Arthur," I whispered.

Arthur jerked his head toward me, then turned back to Warren, tipped his chin toward the ceiling, and breathed air into the man's body. Warren's chest rose and fell, but otherwise was deathly still.

Smack! Arthur hit him again.

"Darn you, Will!" Arthur called. "Get the wagon over to the stairs! Help me get him outta here!"

In a second, I was back down the stairs, running to the team and the wagon. An image of Dr. Wilcox flashed into my mind, the way he had hit Yellowfly on the chest and breathed his own breath into a man I thought was long dead, until me and Arthur had heard him call, "Get a stretcher. He's alive!"

I jumped onto the wagon and slashed the reins across the horses' backs. They bolted down the alley with me screaming "Whoa! Whoa!" and leaning back hard on the reins. When I got them slowed and turned back down the alley, Arthur had his hands under Warren's armpits, his fingers locked across his chest, dragging Warren backward down the stairs, his bare feet bumping from step to step.

Arthur stopped as the far edge of the wagon hooked the fifth stair, lifted it from the ground and the wagon slid under and stopped. He pulled Warren from the stair right out onto the wagon deck.

"Go!" he yelled.

I leaned over the hitch with my legs bent and my rear end hovering over the wooden surface and screamed "He-ah! He-ah!" all the way down Main Street and on over the railway tracks to the Indian hospital.

Behind me came loud smacks and the sound of Arthur breathing for two men.

I Don't Know What to Do

The Indian hospital was about two miles by road from the Grayson beer parlor, near enough that the horses were still wild with running and not far enough away that I could get them stopped with all my pulling on the reins and cussing put together.

A nurse stuck her head out the front door as we came thundering toward her. When she figured I wouldn't run right up the front steps and knock her down, she gave me a hard look that said I was lucky she didn't call the Mounties and have me thrown in jail. Then she saw Arthur and Joe Warren behind the straw bale and disappeared inside.

I turned the team hard to the left, their hooves kicking up chunks of gravel and dirt as they fought the reins. A second later, their heads dropped and the wagon slowed. At the tall grass bordering the hospital grounds, they had nearly stopped.

"Swing 'em around!" Arthur called.

In that moment, with my head turning away from Arthur and back to the horses, I saw Warren's eyes open as they had on Vimy Ridge when Arthur and Wilfred saved his life. They were watching as Arthur breathed air into his body, maybe saving his life one more time.

I had the team turned and headed back to the main entrance when the nurse exploded out the door. A second nurse followed close behind. Then came Dr. Wilcox. They all climbed onto the wagon, hollering words I had never heard before.

Arthur sat down on the straw bale, his back to my back, breathing long, deep breaths like he had run the whole way from the beer parlor.

"Is he —" I asked, not knowing if I should say "dead" or "alive."

"I don't know."

Arthur was off the wagon deck and up the steps, holding the door open before I even figured out I could help in a better way than sitting with my mouth open. Dr. Wilcox had Warren under the arms. The back of Warren's head was resting on the doctor's chest, his neck at a sharp angle, like he was making sure the nurses didn't steal the dirt from under his thick old toenails. But his eyes were closed, and he looked awfully pale. If he wasn't dead, he was darn close.

When Dr. Wilcox gave me his sharp look, I jumped from the wagon, squeezed past the nurses and held open the second set of doors that made the main entrance to the hospital.

In hardly a minute, Warren was on a table with wheels, on his way down the hallway and into a room where I had probably been when I got rushed in on the same wagon, my body burning up from fever made by a German officer's button buried in my shoulder.

Arthur let the outer door fall closed and held on to the railing going down the steps, steadying himself, like he'd spent a chunk of his own life breathing life back into Joe Warren. On the bottom step, he sat, folded his wrists across his knees and rested his forehead on his arms.

I don't know what made me decide we wouldn't be needing the wagon and horses. Maybe it was because it was so late. Maybe it was because I could just as easily sleep on the ground as in my own bed, or maybe it was because Arthur was crying, and I didn't know how to help him. But I led the team over to the grass, unhitched them and tossed the tack on the wagon. The horses wandered off. I broke open the straw bale, spread it on the ground, then fluffed it into a bed big enough for me and Arthur. I set the small bottle of whiskey Emma had given me in the grass on the other side of the wagon's wheel. I didn't want a grownup seeing a thirteen year old with a bottle of whiskey.

Arthur hadn't moved. I didn't like to see him crying. He was stronger than me in every way. Seeing him like this made me afraid.

I walked through the dark to the small side door I'd sneaked out earlier in the week and headed down the hall. There had been a bag of blankets sitting in front of the door with "Laundry" written on it, and there it was again. I left with four dark gray wool blankets. I folded two into the shape of pillows and spread the others as covers.

I was lying there, looking at the starry blackness of night, wondering if all the world was as crazy as Grayson. Then I got a shiver wondering if everything, even up there in the stars, was as crazy.

Then Arthur sat cross-legged on the covers, put his hand on my chest and shook me gently.

"I don't know what to do," he whispered.

I sat up with my back to the wagon's wheel and pulled the blanket up to my chest.

"You don't need to do anything," I said. "I'll get Warren to say Pots killed Wilfred. It doesn't matter if he can remember or not, as long as he says it."

"What if he dies first?"

"I'll go after Pots and make his life so miserable he'll tell the truth just to get rid of me."

Again Arthur rested his head in his hands.

"All I'm saying," I said, "is we'll think of something."

"I don't want to cause any more misery."

"Joe Warren doesn't deserve nothing from you. And Pots deserves even less."

"It doesn't matter what they deserve," Arthur said. "I can't push a man so hard that he'll die."

"Arthur, he's an Indian hater."

"I've been trying to keep him alive since Vimy Ridge. You saw how he looked at me. He's not an Indian hater. He just hates himself."

"I said I'll do it, Arthur. I'll get him to say it was Pots."

Arthur stared at me for a few long seconds. "He's got to do it because he wants to. Or I'll stand against you."

"I'm not your enemy, Arthur."

"Neither is he."

I didn't know what to say. Joe Warren had been drunk for thirty-five years, going all the way back to Vimy Ridge. Maybe it was his way of forgetting. Other men did the same thing. My own dad drank to forget.

When I turned, Arthur was asleep.

I pulled his blanket up to his chin and folded the extra back over his chest where he liked to have a little more warmth.

I lay back and looked up at the stars, trying to imagine what could make an Indian hater and an Indian turn away from what they'd been for their whole lives. The answer didn't come.

I dreamed I was in the sweat lodge with Arthur and Warren, only they didn't know I was there. "You have to want to do this or it won't work," Arthur kept saying. "I don't know what to do," Warren kept whispering back. Then the rolling thunder returned, and we were swept to Vimy Ridge.

Booze Will Do That
to a Man

I was in that place where I'm not really awake or asleep, where the dreams are so crazy a fellow might as well just open his eyes and get on with the day no matter how bad it turns out. The sun was hot on my face when something hard struck the bottom of my foot.

"What the ——" I said, and sat up.

It was Sergeant Findley, the bald Mountie with the big red mustache, now slapping his black billy into his left palm. "There's no camping on government property. And ranging livestock is illegal."

"What?"

"Get those horses hitched," Findley said, "and get a move on, or I'll run the two of you in for trespassing."

While Arthur limped off after the horses, Findley moved his foot under the blanket and rolled it over until he could see the hospital letters sewn into the material.

"I could add theft of government property," he said, running his hand over his mustache, "but then I'd miss my breakfast. Neither of you two are worth that."

I was standing, trying to keep my weight off my sore foot, hoping Sergeant Findley wouldn't find the whiskey bottle hidden in the grass behind the wagon's front tire.

He reached out with his billy club, eased it down my injured shoulder and paused like he knew exactly where the wound was.

The pressure from the stick made my arm feel hot.

"Mr. Howe's got ears all over this town. You oughta be careful whispering your secrets, he might be listening."

"I'm not scared of Old Man Howe."

"Aren't you a goddamned prize," he said. "Mr. Vimy Ridge. Better than all the rest. Out to save old Joe Warren from his own demons."

I pushed the stick from my shoulder and stared at him.

He grinned. "Strong silent type, eh? I want this straw cleaned up and I don't want to see either of you anywhere near this property. Do you hear me?"

I just stood there rubbing my shoulder.

He slid his billy club under his belt and got back in his car. He revved the engine and spun up a rooster tail of gravel, pelting the wagon deck and my back as I turned away and covered my face.

"How's Findley?" Arthur asked, walking through the dust.

"The usual. Mad at everybody about everything."

Arthur hitched the team and listened to me complaining. I stopped talking when Arthur bent under the horse's belly, grabbed a leather strap and gave it a hard pull. The horse let out a long, windy fart that made the hairs on his tail stand nearly straight out.

"I don't know if that was for your complaining or Findley's gravel," Arthur said, grinning up at me.

I flapped the blanket in the air, but it didn't help. A horse's first fart of the day can be as bad as a gas attack on Vimy Ridge.

When I returned the blankets to the laundry bag, I considered sneaking up to see if Warren was still alive, but I heard footsteps coming down the hall, so I headed back outside. I quickly scooped up the straw and tossed it onto the wagon.

We were about to leave when the door swung open and Dr. Wilcox came out. He had black stubble growing on his face, and he looked like he might fall over and sleep right on the ground. When he saw me and Arthur, he got a disappointed look, like he figured he had to talk to us but really wanted to go home instead.

"That straw looks as appealing as anything I've felt under my back in a day and a half," he said.

"You want us to give you a ride home?" I asked.

Dr. Wilcox seemed to blink slower and slower as if my offer and the straw had brought him as close to sleeping as a man could get and still keep standing.

He shook his head very slowly. "I've got a full day in the office ahead of me. Just hope I don't have to save somebody's life." He turned to Arthur. "I don't know where you learned your technique. But if there's thanks coming, he owes you more than he owes me."

Behind us, the door opened and closed again. A few seconds later, a big black car turned in front of the hospital and headed toward town.

Arthur pulled himself up, sat with his legs hanging over the deck and stared at the doctor.

"So he's alive?"

"I've never seen a man brought back from the brink like this. Not from a heart attack as bad as this one."

"We did the right thing then?" Arthur asked. "I mean, bringing him here and that other stuff?"

"Depends if Joe wants to live," he said. "You'll have to ask him yourself."

He patted Arthur's knee, a sorrowful pat that left a soul empty of almost everything but regret.

"Where'd you get medic training?" Dr. Wilcox finally asked. "Sure wasn't at the Indian school."

"It was a long time ago, from a man you never met."

Dr. Wilcox reached his hand under his white doctor's coat, took something from his shirt pocket and handed it to Arthur like he didn't want me to see, like it was a secret just for Arthur.

"Joe gave this to me before the drugs put him to sleep," Dr. Wilcox said. "He said he doesn't remember the person in it, or why he himself is there. He can hardly remember his own life. Booze will do that to a man."

Arthur turned his cupped palm and glanced at the object. When he put it into his shirt pocket, I caught a glimpse of faces, like on an old photograph.

Dr. Wilcox patted Arthur's knee again, a friendly

good-bye pat, then glanced over at me.

"Thanks for the offer," he said. "But if I don't get the car back to my wife, I'll be in for it. No trouble bigger than a woman waiting to go shopping and no car to get her there." He turned from us and half staggered toward a dark blue DeSoto sedan.

We waited until Dr. Wilcox turned north toward town. Being ahead of somebody that sleepy would be a sure way to get run into the ditch.

"What did he give you?" I asked as we walked to the front of the wagon and climbed on.

"Nothing."

"Let me see."

"It doesn't have anything to do with you."

"Then it won't hurt nobody if you show me."

Arthur snapped the reins.

The horses let out a snort and jerked forward, clopping along the gravel surface.

"Come on, Arthur. Maybe I can see something you missed."

"There's nothing there to miss."

I reached for his shirt pocket, but he slapped my hand down. I stared at him for a bit, then stretched out and kicked the right horse in the flank.

The horse jerked hard, and in the next second both horses bolted. While Arthur was leaning back on the reins, I jammed my hand into his shirt pocket.

I pulled out an old photograph.

It was two boys about our age, standing together with a big catch of pike on a stick held between them.

They had a free arm across each other's shoulder. They looked like best friends. Then I saw what Arthur had seen, what Joe Warren couldn't see, or couldn't remember. One boy was Warren, the other was Wilfred Black — Catface's grandpa, Wolfleg.

I stuffed the picture back into Arthur's pocket and stared at the gravel road.

Of all the things Arthur and I had done together as friends, there was nothing better than fishing. It had in it all the best of being friends, sitting on the shore with the warm sun on our skin, sleeping now and then, bragging about the big one, talking about all the things in life that really mattered. That was really why God made fishing, and why best friends always did it.

Something Pretty Bad Must'a Happened

I wouldn't believe that Wilfred Black and Joe Warren had once been friends like Arthur and me were right now. If I did, then I'd have to believe that one day something could happen to make us hate each other.

"How could they go from that picture to what we saw on Vimy Ridge?"

Arthur stared like he wasn't sure who I was, as if I would turn on him at any second. Then he let his chin settle to his chest like he was trying to look into his pocket at the picture he was too afraid to hold.

"I don't know," Arthur finally said. "Only two men know for sure. One is dead. The other's just about dead, and his brain's been eaten up with booze. I don't think he can remember his own name, let alone thirty-five years ago.

"You don't just wake up one morning and start hating your best friend," he said, and made a clicking sound to the horses. "Something made Joe Warren the way he is. Something pretty bad must'a happened."

"I'd never turn on you, Arthur."

"Even if I called you names?"

"You do that now."

"What if I said you'd starve to death if you had to catch fish to live off?"

"That would just be a big lie."

"So what if I said it?"

"That'd be a bad thing to say to a friend," I said. "I'd have to wrestle you 'til you took it back."

Arthur just smiled. He knew he was a better wrestler. He was better at most things. I believe it was because he was closer to being a man than I was.

"What if I stole your girlfriend?"

"Girlfriend?" I said. "You mean one you'd kiss and stuff?"

"Yeah."

"I'd give her to you. I wouldn't have much use for a girl like that."

"What if she was good at making soda biscuits?"

"I might have to wrestle you again, but only if she could make bannock too. And kept lots of strawberry jam around. And had tea with canned milk and sugar."

Arthur grinned and gave my leg a hard slap.

It always made me feel good when Arthur was happy, even if he was really trying to forget what was in his pocket. Arthur was a lot of fun when he wasn't mad at something the white man did or lied about — or photographs that could remind him that some things never change — men die in wars, and Indians and whites don't stay friends.

He gave the reins a quick snap.

"He-ah!" he hollered.

The horses let out a snort and jerked hard on the hitch. The next moment, I was holding on to the wooden deck to keep from falling backward.

When the horses got to a speed they liked, Arthur gave them another snap of the reins, and off they went as hard as they had when they hauled Warren to the Indian hospital. Their tails rose up slightly, like a poop was coming. It was just how they got when they were running like nature had intended, but sometimes a fellow had to be ready to duck. It happened to horses when they were having fun. Running and pooping.

I've Lived It Every Day

A big black Dodge car was parked in front of Arthur's house.

"Who's that?" Arthur asked.

"Looks like Jane Howe's car," I said. "Emma's sister."

"What's she want here?"

"I don't know," I said. "But I expect it's important."

"I don't like white people coming to my house."

I gave Arthur a stare that looked worse than it really was.

"I didn't mean you. You're not really white."

We unhitched the horses, pumped two buckets full of water and set them side by side against the house so the horses could drink and not kick the buckets over.

Arthur gave the black Dodge a hard stare. "Figure she's inside?"

"I could look under the car and see if she's changing the oil."

"You don't have to get smart."

"Come on, Arthur, Jane's the librarian. Maybe she's here because you forgot to return a book."

"Don't think so," Arthur said. "I've never been in a library."

"You don't read?"

"Not unless it's about Indians."

"She's got Treaty Number 7 hanging on the wall. I've read it myself, got to be six times now."

"I don't need to read that thing," Arthur said. "I've lived it every day."

"Okay, I don't want to talk about the treaty. We always get into a fight over that thing."

Arthur pulled the photograph from his shirt pocket, held it to my face, then stuffed it into my pocket.

"What was that for?"

"You want to know what can wreck a friendship?"

"No, I don't."

"Lies," Arthur said. "Seventy-five years of them."

"Jeez, Arthur, I didn't write the darn treaty. And I sure as heck didn't make nobody sign the thing."

Arthur always said the Xs on the treaty, the ones the Indian chiefs were supposed to have made, all looked made by the same hand, like somebody had put the mark next to their names no matter if they agreed or not. When it came to Treaty Number 7, everything was a lie to Arthur.

He stood on the railway tie that made their front step and stomped his feet as if he'd just walked through horse poop and was trying not to drag in the mess. But I knew he was just warning those inside that he was coming in, maybe letting them know he wasn't too happy about a white person's car being parked in front of his door.

Old Drunk Joe

Arthur's house was cramped, with hardly enough light coming from the two small windows to read a book of any kind. A flame flickered from the stacked river stones and metal grates of the cooking fire. Three women sat at the table staring at me and Arthur.

It was very hot.

Arthur's mom sat at the middle of her yellow-topped table, Emma sat at the right end and Jane sat at the left end. There were tin cups in front of them and a big steaming pot of tea.

Nobody said anything, so I figured it must be my turn. I put my hand into my shirt pocket and took out the picture.

"I don't know," I said, pretending to be an expert on something I knew nothing about, "if I was Joe Warren, I'd've stayed friends with my bottle and never mind bothering a fellow like Wilfred Black."

Arthur made a sound like he had something stuck in his throat.

"Old Drunk Joe." I shook my head. "He most likely lied about something to get Wilfred on his side. Must'a been a whopper to make Wilfred figure Old Joe was a friend."

"Shut up," Arthur whispered.

Now Arthur's mom and Jane were staring at Emma. She raised her hand from where she'd been gripping her teacup as if she was shushing them, saying it's okay, he's just a fool.

"Why don't you boys sit?" Emma said. "I'd like to tell you something about Joe Warren."

"I already know," I said. "He's in a bad way. Dr. Wilcox said his heart stopped. He said it was all those years of drinking. Arthur saved him."

She nodded slowly. "I know all that. Jane talked to Dr. Wilcox this morning."

We sat together, me beside Emma and Arthur beside Jane, all quiet like we were in church, waiting for the sermon to begin.

"I went to school with Joe," Emma finally said. "I knew by the way he watched me that he liked me the way boys like girls after they reach a certain age. He was a decent person, but I didn't like him back. Not in that way."

I could feel her looking at me but I had my head down. I didn't want to see the truth in her eyes. If I could've blocked the sound of her voice, I would have.

"I had my eye on another fellow. Someone tall and strong and handsome. It was Joe's friend I wanted."

Her voice broke, and the room felt as still as a funeral parlor.

"But I went with Joe. I pretended to like him in that way. It worked. I got close to his friend. The one I really wanted."

She put her hand on mine. Her touch left my hand wet with her tears. When I looked up, I turned to Arthur first. He was turned away like he was crying.

"I lied to Joe," she said.

She took the photograph from my hand and held it to her chest.

"I was a fool. I didn't see what I was doing to him, coming between friends, choosing one over the other."

I just sat, trying to think of what to do. There was hardly a sound coming from anybody that wasn't a sniffle. I decided I'd wait for someone else to talk. But I kept wondering why Jane and Emma were there, why any of this mattered to me and Arthur, except to make Emma feel better for telling it. That usually worked for me.

Then something came to me, something from what Emma had done to Warren all those years ago. Maybe she could go back to him one more time, pretending she cared about him again, and get him to tell what Pots did on Vimy Ridge.

I filled the lone tin cup sitting by the teapot and drank it in long, hot gulps, letting it burn all the way into the center of my body to punish such a horrible thought.

I was still waiting for someone to talk when Jane

pushed her chair back and stood.

"Will, Arthur. We better get going."

In a breath, Arthur was standing.

"I've got to take the team back to Watcher," Arthur said.

"The horses won't go anywhere," Jane said.

When she opened the door and the bright sunlight spilled in, Arthur's mom had Emma's head on her shoulder, gently stroking her hair like my mom did for me when no amount of talking could stop the hurting in my heart.

They Saved a Man's Life

I watched the back of Jane's head as she drove. Her hair was light brown like mine, only hers had gray in it, maybe every other hair.

Arthur set his hands on the front seat next to Jane and pulled himself forward until he had his chin nearly resting on the seat back.

"Where're you taking us?" he asked. "Those horses need to be washed down. They need to be treated like they saved a man's life."

She lifted one hand from the steering wheel and, without looking back, patted Arthur's forearm.

"Catface wants to see you two. He's at the Indian hospital. We dropped him off this morning."

"That's kind'a important," Arthur said. "How come nobody said nothing about Catface 'til we're almost there?"

"I wanted to hear what you cared about," she said.

"I care about those horses."

"And that they saved a life," she added. "I assume from that that you also care about that life."

"So."

The inside of the Dodge smelled of soap and a little of perfume, like ladies smell in the morning. I wondered if Arthur noticed that about Jane or just that she was white.

"What would you've done if I didn't say nothing?" he asked.

"I would have driven all over the reserve until you did."

"What if I said I hated Joe Warren for all his years of hating Indians, for nearly killing Yellowfly, for doing nothing when he knew Pots killed Wolfleg on Vimy Ridge?"

"I hate him for those things, too," she said, and turned the car onto the hospital grounds.

Arthur gave the seat a hard push and flopped back, where I was trying to find something out the side window worth talking about so I didn't have to hear the silence.

I Couldn't Stop Him

Joe Warren was in the same room I'd been in when I got my shoulder wounded on Vimy Ridge. I wondered if this room was left open for white people who couldn't take the chance of dying in the ambulance on the way to the white hospital in Calgary. Then I wondered if this room was for Vimy Ridge veterans.

The nurse held the door open, but instead of letting us in, she reached across the opening and took a tight grip on the jamb.

Though I was behind Arthur, I could still see Warren lying flat on his back, his big feet making two tall bumps in the hospital blanket, his chest fluttering under quick shallow breaths, his gray and black whiskers shaved clean like he was ready for the grave, his skin the color of chalk.

He didn't look to me like a man full of hate.

"If you make any noise," the nurse said, "I'll have to ask you to leave."

"We're not staying long," Arthur said. "If we could get Catface to come out, we wouldn't even go in."

Catface sat in the corner farthest from the foot of

the bed, his long arms folded across his chest, his eyes with the same dark stare I'd seen in the photograph of Wilfred Black.

"We'll be quiet," I said.

She nodded and lowered her arm.

"How's the shoulder?" she asked.

"Hardly think about it."

I didn't want to be anywhere near Old Joe, so I hugged the wall and inched my way to the window and pretended like I was interested in how fast the poplar trees were turning yellow. When Catface got up from the chair, I worked my way under the picture of the young queen and sat. The chair felt so warm I figured Catface must have sat here the whole time since he arrived.

I pushed the chair back tight to the wall and cupped my hand over the wound on my shoulder.

"Why'd you come here?" Arthur asked from the door. "I thought you were supposed to stay with your grandma."

"I had a dream that I was in the sweat lodge with him," Catface said, moving toward Warren. "Wolfleg was there, too. That they sat together like friends."

Arthur moved to the foot of Warren's bed. "You had a vision?"

"Early this morning," Catface said. "Then just after sunrise, Jane drove up in her Dodge. She told Grandma what you and Will did for Warren. She said most of the town knew after Mr. Phillips heard you two hollering and screaming as you raced a team of horses through town after midnight. Then Grandma told me the other part that I'd seen in my dream."

Now Arthur was standing next to Catface. They whispered in Blackfoot. Arthur began rolling up the empty sleeve. Catface held the material snug to the base of Warren's missing arm.

Warren's eyes opened then closed. His head turned slightly at the sound of the Blackfoot voices. In the next second, his eyes were wide open, his chest heaving in big gulps of air.

Catface placed his hand lightly on Warren's chest.

"Don't worry," Catface said, "we're just fixing up your arm."

Warren stared at those eyes that looked so much like Wilfred Black, when they had been young and friends. His breathing slowed and he turned and stared at the ceiling, then saw me sitting in the far corner, my hand moving slowly over the wound on my shoulder.

In that moment, I felt frozen back in that trench on Vimy Ridge, my back pushed up tight to the wall and Pots sitting in the mud not five feet away, Warren's eyes trying to make some sense of even the smallest piece of time.

Arthur slid a safety pin into the folded sleeve bottom. As if Arthur had jabbed his stump, Warren sat straight up, his eyes as round as a china teacup, as clear and cold as river water in winter.

"You could'a stopped this," Warren said, and jerked the hospital tube from his arm.

I turned to where Pots should have been sitting. When I tried to stand, Warren was on me, pulling me to the floor as he grabbed at the imaginary rifle that Pots was readying to fire.

Warren screamed a threat to Pots that could have traveled all the way to Vimy Ridge, his blood running down his arms where the tube had been inside his body, smeared his blood across my face as his good arm grabbed me around the neck, his stump punching widely at my face.

He hollered and cussed.

In a second, Catface and Arthur had Warren by the shoulders, pulling him back and falling against the steel frame of the bed.

The door flew open and hit the wall with a sharp bang, like somebody'd fired a rifle inside the room.

"What in the living God are you three doing?" Dr. Wilcox shouted. "Get up and get out!"

"But I didn't do anything," I said. "It was Warren. He went crazy."

Dr. Wilcox and the nurse pushed past us.

"I said get out."

Arthur and Catface were up and out the door before I could stand. When I caught the door and pulled it open, they had already disappeared down the stairs. I limped down the hallway with my hand clamped tightly on my shoulder. Behind me, Joe Warren was trying to talk over the jerking sobs coming from deep inside him.

"Awww, God!" he called out. "I couldn't stop him."

I Want a Drink

Arthur and Catface were just disappearing into the line of tall poplars that formed the border between the hospital property and the reserve to the west.

"Hey!" I called.

They didn't even pause.

"You can't leave me here."

When I broke through the tall grass and weeds and trees and came out onto the reserve, Arthur and Catface were already halfway to the clump of trees and the small slough where Arthur's grandpa and Watcher were doing a sweat lodge.

I sat at the edge of the prairie grass. If I'd any strength left, I might've run after them or called out again.

But I had nothing left.

The sun was well past midday, but still hot and high in the late August sky when I heard the footsteps moving among the trees and grass behind me. Joe Warren came out from the border of woods and stared down at me. He still wore the long-sleeved pajama top with one sleeve rolled up and pinned in place and the other cut off to allow the tube to connect to his body, but now he'd pulled on a pair of pants. The zipper was still open and the pajama top hung out the opening. His feet were bare and he swayed in a regular circular pattern. In most other ways, he looked as normal as every other person in Grayson. The brown snuff-spit that always ran down his chin had been wiped clean, and his eyes had stopped jerking around as if he was trying to make sense of ordinary things and faces.

Still I didn't trust him not to get some crazy memory from Vimy Ridge and attack me.

"You want to sit?" I asked as I slowly inched away from him.

"I want a drink."

"I've got whiskey," I said. "Emma Howe gave me a full bottle for you."

"She always knew how to get to me."

I wondered if Dr. Wilcox had a shot that made a forgetful brain start working again.

Warren held out his hand no higher than a fellow swinging his arm if he was walking slowly.

"I'll take it," he said.

I guess I'd never stood this close to Joe Warren before. If I had, I'd have noticed how tall he was, maybe a whole foot taller than me, and I was about average for thirteen.

He wiggled his fingers to hurry me along.

"You got to wait 'til I do something."

"I've been waiting my whole life," he said. "What are you making me wait on now?"

"Pee."

He glanced down at his open zipper. He shook his head and stuffed the length of pajama top back in, but left the zipper down.

"Do it right here."

"I'd rather go in the trees."

He waved his hand at thigh height and tried not to fall over.

"I know you," he finally said. "You're that Samson kid. I tried to kick your head off awhile back."

"You missed."

I guess he'd already forgotten about trying to strangle me in the hospital room.

I headed through the border of trees and around to the tall grass where Arthur and I had slept. The mickey of whiskey was right where I'd left it.

"What's that you've got there, boy?" When I turned, Sergeant Findley was just coming out the front door of the hospital.

"It's nothing," I said.

"Looks like illegal liquor."

"It's tea. Mom made me some tea."

He moved to the bottom of the stairs and started down the gravel trail toward me.

"You seen that old drunk, Joe Warren?" Findley asked. "Dr. Wilcox says he gave him a shot of something to knock him out, but it worked like booze and woke him right up. Now he's run off."

"I never saw him."

"Wilcox said you and your Indian friends were here tormenting the old fool. Maybe you slipped him a mickey of hard stuff. Is that what's got his heart pumping again?"

I stuffed the bottle in my pants pocket and took off.

"Why you son of a —" Sergeant Findley said behind me.

I ran to where the hospital entrance entered the main road. Behind me, I heard his car door slam and the engine roar to life. I was already down the road fifty yards, heading to town, and had dropped flat in the tall ditch grass when Findley's car came tearing out onto the road, shooting gravel and dirt all over my back.

I waited until he turned the corner for town, then stood and dusted myself off. When I got back to where I'd left Warren, he was gone.

Warrior's Cry

Sergeant Findley drove slowly along the road heading west toward Arthur's house as if he was expecting me to pop out of the ditch. I backed into the trees and worked my way in the opposite direction, whispering Warren's name as I went. I got fifty yards, turned toward the hospital and sneaked along the edge of the trees. I kept glancing at the rear of the hospital in case Dr. Wilcox came out and caught me.

No one came.

Not even Joe Warren.

I turned back to where I'd left him, stared out across the prairie grass, past the quiet sweat lodge and on to Arthur's house.

Sergeant Findley stood in the packed dirt yard, his car door wide open and his big arm resting on the roof.

Not forty yards away from me, in a dip in the ground, something moved. It was a piece of cloth — Warren's pajama top.

A second later, Joe was trying to stand.

He got to his hands and knees, fell forward and disappeared. Whatever Dr. Wilcox had put into him had started to work on Old Joe. When he tried to stand again, I shot out from behind the trees, jumped for him and knocked him flat on his back.

He hardly made a sound except to cuss himself for not remembering to bring some booze. I'd hardly been gone for thirty minutes and he was back to his old self.

He got a pained look on his face as he rubbed the heel of his hand hard over his heart, like there was something terrible happening inside him. A second later, he let out a long, loud burp, smiled up at the heavens and let his eyes fall closed.

I draped my leg across his stomach to keep him from trying to stand again. When his breathing became long and deep, I rolled away, my face just far enough ahead of his tall feet to keep me from passing out from the smell.

I was glad to have the breeze in my favor.

I saw Sergeant Findley pull up to the sweat lodge and get out of his car. He reached down and pulled the flap open, letting the sun's rays in.

In a minute, Sergeant Findley had Watcher, Arthur's grandpa, Catface and Arthur standing naked beside his Mountie's car, as the steam and heat and smoke seeped out of the lodge, took the form of a bull buffalo and drifted east with the breeze.

Findley bent over and stared inside. When he found neither me nor Warren, he pushed the Indian men away from the car, got in, slammed the door and moved off.

First came a loud scream, like an old-time warrior's

cry. Then something heavy boomed against metal. A second later came the sound of bursting glass. I lifted myself to my elbows in time to see Sergeant Findley spin the car around. I stared through the smashed back window as Findley dropped flat across his seat. Watcher's third rock landed right where Findley's head had been. It seemed to push the windshield in for a long time before it exploded through, with shards of glass raining over Findley.

I stood with a jerk and grabbed Joe Warren under the arms, dragging him into the trees. I thought I'd just take him back to the hospital. But I couldn't give him to Sergeant Findley, with Findley all fired up to lay into him for wandering off and breaking some big hospital rule. Findley didn't need a reason that had anything to do with the law or justice. Meanness was good enough for him. Before I set Warren down, I realized he'd been helping me move him, pushing hard against the ground with his heels as I dragged him.

His eyes had the same look as they'd had on Vimy Ridge, when he seemed not to know who was helping him or hurting him.

The smell of Grandpa's smoke, the ancient medicine of the sweat lodge that Findley had let out, drifted around us.

"Take me there," Warren whispered. "I don't want this anymore. I want to go."

I dragged his limp body along the tree line until I reached a dense thicket nearer the lodge. There, I put him in a shallow depression, covered him with dry grass and large, loose leaves. I backtracked and covered all the signs that I'd been there. Unless somebody was a serious tracker, they'd walk right past.

Before I crawled under the covering of dead grass beside Warren, I saw Watcher, his arms handcuffed behind his wide, bare back as Sergeant Findley pushed him into the rear seat of the Mountie car.

I Want to Go!

I prayed that Joe Warren would not die there under grass and leaves with sun filtering across his face as if there was still something good inside him. I prayed he would finally remember there was something worth doing in this life.

He started shivering, so I wiggled out of my shirt and covered his chest. When the shivers passed, he began dreaming, making low screaming sounds, kicking and thrashing and hitting at things that weren't real for the rest of the world.

"Rats!" he shouted. "Get 'em off me! I want to go!"

I clamped my hand over his mouth.

From down along the trees, I could hear Findley's car roll up parallel to where we were lying and stop.

Warren bit down hard on my hand. I clenched my teeth, shook my hand and pressed it tight to my leg. Inside my pocket, I could feel the whiskey bottle's smooth surface.

"He's here someplace," Findley said. "I can smell him."

I pulled out the bottle and unscrewed the cap.
Warren's eyes opened. I slid my arm under his neck
and cradled him like a baby. He took the bottle
between his lips and swallowed two quick gulps. When
I pulled the bottle away, it was half empty.

We lay there until Sergeant Findley's shadow
crossed through the trees, stopped over us and stood
like he knew we were there but had decided to let us
sweat a little. Then a loud booming sound came from
the car. Watcher must have been drumming on the
inside of the car's roof with his feet. Behind it came his
Blackfoot song about the buffalo hunt, thundering like
the hooves of the herd.

Sergeant Findley cussed and crashed through the
trees back to the car.

In the cradle of my arm, Joe Warren slept like a
baby.

I wished I could call out to Watcher, thank him for
protecting us from Sergeant Findley. Then I wondered
what Watcher would think if he saw me holding Old
Drunk Joe, the Indian hater, if he'd think I'd gone too
far. That didn't last more than a second. I knew
Watcher would just smile the smile that was always
there to be given freely to anybody who did what was
right.

We lay there until the sun had slipped below the
western horizon. Then I heard familiar voices, heading
toward us.

"Where do you figure he's gone?" Catface asked.

"Someplace not here," Arthur said.

"I think he's out here waiting 'til the trouble's gone."

"Then what? He'll come have a sweat?"

"Sure, why not?"

"I know him better than you do," Arthur said.

"So tell me then."

"He's likely followed Findley to the jail and he's working on a plan to break out Watcher. And I don't believe he'll go anywhere near a sweat lodge as long as he lives."

Arthur was right about that last part.

I pushed off the grass and leaves, got Warren to standing, draped his arm across my shoulder and headed out toward Arthur and Catface as if Warren was a wounded soldier and I was his friend.

It Was Joe Warren Who Was Running

Joe Warren was doing his best to imitate Watcher's Blackfoot song about the buffalo hunt. The sounds came from deep inside him, like real Indian language. Maybe Old Joe could actually speak Blackfoot. Maybe he had come as close to being an Indian as I had. Thinking that made me wonder if Grayson was a disease a fellow caught when he grew up.

"Where'd you get him?" Arthur asked. "You know kidnapping is against the law. No wonder Findley's hunting for you."

They took his weight from my shoulders, Arthur where I had been and Catface holding Warren around the waist on the side where his arm was missing.

"He smells like dead leaves and old whiskey," Arthur said.

"The rats! Get 'em off me!" Warren called and struggled weakly. "I want to go. Why don't you let me go back?"

Ahead of us, in the growing night, I could see the glow of the fire that heated the river stones, the shape of Arthur's grandpa as he slid the long-handled shovel into the red glow, retrieve a stone and move it to the pit at the center of the sweat lodge.

"I'm not going in," I said. "You can't make me go back there." My voice came out sounding like Joe Warren.

A shiver crept up my spine.

What would he do on Vimy Ridge? Had the rats been crawling over him every day that the booze ran low? Did he want to kill that ugly, gnawing memory that ate at his heart?

Arthur's grandpa was holding the buffalo-robe flap back against the dome of the sweat lodge as if he'd been expecting us. I had to run to catch up to Arthur and Catface.

"Slow down!" I called. "What's all the hurry?"

"We can't stop him," Arthur said.

I saw then that it was Joe Warren who was running, staggering from side to side. Arthur and Catface were only keeping him going in a straight line. At twenty yards from the sweat lodge, Old Joe pushed free from their grip.

Arthur's grandpa stood quiet, naked in the cool night.

Warren stopped so close I was afraid Grandpa would have to hug him to keep him from falling over. But Warren stood straight and tall, listening closely to the Blackfoot words spoken to him. Warren glanced over his shoulder at me and the bottle of whiskey I had in my hand, then took the pipe and sacred plants from Grandpa's hands and entered the lodge.

When he reemerged, he had the same look on his face that I had that night: Had he made a mistake? Had he put things in the wrong place?

I felt myself inching farther from the sweat lodge, the sound of guns rumbling in my head like thunder, the sting of wind-driven sleet on my face and the burning taste of blood oozing from the chlorine gas blisters in my lungs. I almost ran, but then Warren spoke, imitating Grandpa's Blackfoot words so completely I thought Grandpa must have spoken them.

God's Sweat Lodge

Arthur sat on the ground near the sweat lodge. I sat cross-legged beside him, my hands resting uneasy on my knees, like I was afraid something greater than anything living would crawl out and force me back inside, where the Indian smoke made a fellow live his nightmares.

"Don't breathe the smoke," I whispered to myself. "Don't smoke the pipe. And don't ask for a prayer. You might get it."

"Are you praying?" Arthur asked.

"Just thinking."

"Do you have to do it so loud?"

"No matter what," I said, "Arthur and I will still be friends. In all that happens to us, this will never change."

Arthur blinked. "I believe I just heard you thinking again."

"I was praying."

"You might get that one."

Behind us, the heat from the fire had died down to nearly nothing. All around, the night hung cool and still.

We watched Catface's hands moving between the earth and flap of buffalo robe as he blocked the light from the outside world.

When Arthur started to get up, I jerked my hand out and grabbed his wrist. "Don't leave me here."

"I gotta go pee."

I followed and peed even though I didn't have to.

Arthur stood staring at the black dome of stars.

"What's that one called again?" Arthur asked, and turned his head slightly to the north.

"The Big Dipper."

"Oh, yeah. That was kind'a easy."

"A blind man could'a got that one."

Arthur shifted his stare to the imaginary line where the sun had passed two hours earlier.

"And that one?" He was looking at Venus.

"It's a planet."

"I was just testing you," he said, and turned back.

I touched his arm again, stopping him before I had to say out loud that I didn't want to be anywhere near the sweat lodge and hear the screams of the dying men on Vimy Ridge. I didn't want to smell the dead rats. I didn't want to breathe gas that carried the stinging death.

"You know what Grandpa calls all those stars stuck on that black dome?" Arthur asked.

"No."

"God's sweat lodge."

"Oh?"

"When He does a sweat, He makes a volcano and lets the oceans flow in to get steam."

"He does this at night?"

"He makes the night."

"What about the sacred plants? And the pipe?"

"That came when the fire moved to the land. God let man smell the smoke from the forests and the prairies. He showed His people how to see Him."

"That isn't really true, Arthur. You're making this stuff up."

He just stared up at that giant dome covering all of the world. "Come on," he said, and slapped my leg, "let's go back to those hot ashes. I'm getting cold."

"I think they're already dead."

"I'll stir them up and throw on some dry grass. We'll get warm."

"I don't want to go there."

"We're already in God's sweat lodge."

Arthur reached out his long, muscular arm like he had that day seven years ago when he rescued me from the gang of Indian boys. I grabbed his forearm and he grabbed mine. And again I remembered the touch his hand left on me, that if two kids could stay friends forever, they would be us.

He Talks To Ground

Arthur fell asleep almost right away, leaving me to tend the embers he'd found smoldering under the heap of ash. There were just enough bits of kindling left from Grandpa's fire to make a small flame and get a poplar log burning. It wasn't a big fire but it kept the chill off.

Arthur lay flat on his back, prairie grass stuffed into his boots, making a U-shaped pillow. He made little puffing sounds as his sleep became deep and peaceful.

Nothing seemed to bother Arthur much right now. It was like everything was going as planned, but I didn't know whose plan it was — Arthur's were mostly like mine, and mine was to see what happened and then figure out how to get out of the mess I was in because I didn't have a plan in the first place. I guess I was afraid that somebody or something inside the sweat lodge was making the plan for all of us, even Catface and Old Joe.

I looked up at the big dome of God's sweat lodge and said a quick prayer that I wouldn't do the wrong thing because I had missed all the things He'd tried to show me in my life, and that whatever finally came crawling out of the sweat lodge, I'd know if I should follow it or run the other way.

I tried to lie down, but my eyes wouldn't stay closed, the fire would crack and a spark jump out at me. I sat up, facing the sweat lodge with my legs crossed, like an old-time Indian.

Arthur's grandpa had been inside for nearly two hours. It must have been close to midnight and I still hadn't heard Grandpa's big Blackfoot voice, or smelled the smoke from the sacred plants as they flashed on the glowing river rocks, or caught the bitter taste of the pipe, or heard men cry out as spirits visited their souls. But I still saw my own time in the sweat lodge. I saw Warren lying in the mud at the bottom of a German trench, fat yellow-toothed rats crawling up his legs and arm and chest, his bloody stump swinging helplessly in the air. Pots stared back, his Lee-Enfield rifle still hot with murder, Wilfred Black facedown in the mud at Warren's side, Pots whispering, then talking louder and louder. "I saved your miserable life, Joe Warren. You will remember this moment with every breath you draw."

I pulled the whiskey bottle from my pants pocket, unscrewed the cap and took a mouthful. I had to swallow hard three times, but I kept it down. A ball of fire lifted from my middle and rushed to my head, and I was grinning. When the rats turned from Warren and moved across the mud to Pots, I quietly cheered them on. As they swarmed him, he drew his pistol and began shooting down his legs, missing the rats but shooting off his toes until he had none left. Now I was laughing so hard I'd stopped breathing. Then Pots turned to me, his face twisted in pain, but it wasn't Pots holding the smoking pistol. It was me.

I vomited on the ground between my hands.

Behind me, I heard the sound of the buffalo robe flop back against the dome, someone worked his way out of the opening, then the robe flopped back. Grandpa's big bare feet stopped at my side as I vomited the last of the whiskey.

"Now I call you He Talks To Ground."

I wiped my shirt sleeve under my nose.

Grandpa dipped an old rag into a bucket of water and washed the sweat from his body. When he was finished, he poured some water over his head, then set the bucket on the ground next to me.

"Wash," he said. "You smell like a drunk."

Arthur was just waking. He sat for a second and stared at me then up at Grandpa.

"Where are they?" he asked. "Is it done? Are they back?"

Grandpa grunted and dressed.

"Well?" Arthur asked me.

"I didn't see anything but Grandpa."

"Jeez, Will," Arthur said, "you smell bad."

"I feel worse."

I dunked the rag into the bucket of water and washed my face hard and fast. Arthur was holding his nose when Grandpa came back.

"Give me the whiskey."

I handed the mickey to Grandpa. The bottle almost disappeared in his large brown hands. He unscrewed the cap and poured the whiskey onto the fire. It blazed blue and orange.

"That's what it does to your guts," he said, and let the empty bottle drop next to the cap. "Too much whiskey and I'll call you He Sleeps Under Ground Like Indian."

He headed into the night.

"What do you want us to do?" I called after him and picked up the bottle.

"Go to sleep," he said. "Don't bother me with foolishness."

When I looked back, Arthur was staring at me.

"Now what?"

"You drank over half a bottle of whiskey?"

I didn't say anything about Warren drinking most of it. If I was going to feel so sick, I might as well have had a good reason, even if it was a lie.

"I was just trying to forget," I said. "For a while it worked. Then it all came back up."

When I finally fell asleep, I dreamed I was half buried in a pile of empty booze bottles. Indian men laughed and joked and sang dirty songs. As dawn broke, the men were fighting.

A Rat from Vimy Ridge

I woke the next morning to the sound of men hollering and cussing, but once I got my eyes fully open, it was silent, like the arguing had just been part of my dreams.

Joe Warren stood facing the sweat lodge, pulling his pants up over his bare rear end. Catface was just coming out of the lodge opening. His eyes were as red as hot embers. His cheeks, where his tears had flowed, had been burned and scabbed over. His nose was swollen nearly closed. His lips were puffy and cracked, bits of skin hung in flakes. I prayed he looked that way because he'd been fighting with Warren, but I was afraid it was worse than that.

Catface took a long, wheezing breath as he dragged himself up Warren's arm and pulled on his pants. "Cuss me all you like, I'm still coming with you," he said, and put his hand over his mouth to hide the cough rumbling in his chest. "You can't stop me."

"You've taken a chest full of chlorine gas," Warren said, his arm around Catface's waist. "You're a damned fool. You need to go to the hospital. And as far as cussin' goes, you ain't heard nothing yet."

"I'm coming with you."

Warren snapped his head around. His face was covered in a heavy gray and black beard. I'd never seen three weeks of hair grow overnight. Indian smoke.

"Dammit!" Warren hollered at us. "Help me here. Can't you see he's been gassed? What kind'a friends are you?"

Arthur jumped up and took Catface around the waist. His arm and Warren's arm crossed behind Catface's back.

Warren nodded me over. "Somebody's gotta hold me," he said. "Looks like you lose."

It didn't bother me at all to put my arm around his waist.

"I'd take yours," he said, "but I can't reach."

"It's okay."

"Say," he nearly whispered, "you wouldn't have a sip of whiskey for a fellow?"

"That stuff can kill you."

"I'm not worried about dying. I don't have more than an hour or two left in me. If whiskey shortens it, all the better for the world."

"Okay," Catface finally said. "I'm ready."

"No, you're not," Warren said.

"I'm going."

With that, we headed toward Grayson, all four of us, each with arms locked around the other's waist, Catface and Warren naked from the waist up, their feet bare.

"I'm going to kill him." Catface cleared his chest.

"Brave talk for a fellow with burned-out lungs."

"As long as I don't have to chase him far, I'll be able to do it."

"You'll have to wait in line," Warren said, gentle, like a friend.

"I don't think we should kill anybody," I said. "We should just tell Sergeant Findley everything we all know. Now that we got an eyewitness, he'll throw Pots in jail for sure. And maybe Pots will tell everyone Old Man Howe gave him money to go all the way to Vimy Ridge to kill Wilfred Black, just to keep him from coming home and claiming his land and Howe's daughter. Then we'll get Old Man Howe, too. I'd like to see them two swinging from a government rope."

Warren started laughing first, then Catface, but he had to stop because he couldn't breathe and laugh at the same time. Arthur didn't do anything but look past them both.

"Shut up, Will."

"I just meant —"

Arthur gave me a hard stare.

Now it was clear to me that their plan didn't include me, at least not if I wasn't ready to commit murder.

I adjusted my hand on Warren's cold, damp flesh. As we walked, his stump bumped against my shoulder like he was swinging his arm like normal. I wondered if he could still feel a hand at the end of it. I'd heard that sometimes when a person loses a part of themselves they keep feeling it in its old place, the way they used to. I wondered if Warren was feeling the missing piece of his heart, the one that was whole when he and Wilfred were still friends.

Nothing seemed to make sense anymore. In the old days, all you had to do was look at a man's skin and you could tell if he was good or bad. Then along comes Arthur saying that isn't how it works. So I accepted that I was wrong all my life, and all of Grayson had been, too. But at least I knew which of us is good and which of us is bad. Then along comes Grandpa and his darn Indian smoke and Arthur's ideas about God's sweat lodge, saying something different again, saying maybe Joe Warren is both good and bad, and to understand the man's deeds, we must understand the man.

Now I didn't know nothing about nothing, but at least now I knew I didn't know. I guess I was one up on all the rest.

I decided to stop right there, before I burst a blood vessel, and went to work on a plan. Once we got close enough to town for me to sprint the last two hundred yards, I'd lean hard into Warren and push him and Catface over onto Arthur, then I'd hit for town. By the time Arthur got out from under the pile, I'd have warned Pots and the town and maybe even called Sergeant Findley. I couldn't see any other way. I wasn't going to let murder happen, not even to Pots. I wanted

Pots to get what he deserved, but I remembered how sick Arthur felt when he thought he'd killed him. I didn't want to see that in anyone's eyes as long as I lived.

But I did wonder what Warren and Catface had seen in the Indian smoke in the sweat lodge, what had happened to Catface that left his lungs blistered with chlorine gas, and what they had seen or done together to have them walking with their arms around each other's waists like friends.

When Catface lifted his head from coughing, I saw an image of a man I'd only seen in an old photograph, the man standing with his arm around Emma Howe. The eyes were the same as Wilfred's, but the face had been aged with gas and the memory of Vimy Ridge.

As we got closer to Grayson and the point where I'd decided I'd make my move, I started puffing hard and complaining about the load I had to carry.

"You lookin' for a reason to run?" Arthur said, like he could read my mind. "Because if that's what you want, then do it and stop making a fool of yourself."

"I just meant I was getting tired is all. Jeez, Arthur."

"Shut up, Will."

Warren rubbed his stump across my head and messed up my hair.

"I can smell death in the air," he said. "I only wish I had a sip of whiskey. I'd like to go with something warm inside me."

I put my hand on the outside of my pocket and felt the smooth glass through the material. My mouth filled up with saliva that was bitter with memory, forcing me to swallow twice, then spit on the ground anyway.

We crossed the mound of rocks that held the railway tracks and headed through the layer of dust in Happy Valley, none of us slowing to look at the spot where Joe Warren and Woody Loewan and Pots had tried to kill Yellowfly during my last week of grade six, when I was still a kid. We turned down the alley past the war memorial and in no more than a moment in a bad dream, we were standing, still holding on to one another, in the middle of Main Street, staring through the new plateglass window at Pots sitting behind the desk where he sold insurance for prices people could barely pay.

Catface held back the cough that had been threatening.

Arthur was as silent as a corpse.

Warren's skin had gone so cold under my touch that my hand felt numb.

"Anything left in that bottle?" he whispered. "All I need is a sip."

I pulled the bottle from my pocket and turned it in disbelief. The tea-colored liquid was still halfway up the bottle, as if Grandpa had not poured out a single drop.

Warren let go of Catface and took it from my hand. Before he could swallow a drop, Pots swiveled his desk chair toward us, his big, yellow teeth grinning like a rat from Vimy Ridge.

Beside me, I could feel Warren's body shaking, not from a lack of whiskey, but from the thirty-five years the rats and Vimy Ridge had gnawed at his soul.

Now, Pots stood in his open doorway, his hands folded behind his back, rocking slowly on the heels of his cowboy boots.

"What a sorry-looking bunch," he said. "Hardly worth getting out of my chair. Same old Joe. Never far from his best friend."

When it seemed like we might stand there forever with the August sun cooking us in the street and Pots waiting in the shade of his doorway, I dropped my arm from Warren's side and moved toward the sidewalk.

"Still the coward, Joe?" Pots asked. "You've got kids and your bottle with you. Surely you can find some courage here."

I glanced at the three of them standing together. Arthur seemed like he hoped God would cast Pots into the fire used to heat the rocks of His sweat lodge. Catface's breathing had become so thick he didn't seem long for this earth. And Warren's head kept sinking lower and lower as Pots's words wore him down to the man he'd been for the past thirty-five years.

I turned back to Pots. "I came to warn you. They're coming to get you for the things you done on Vimy Ridge. You better call Sergeant Findley, then run and hide someplace because they're going to kill you, if they can."

"You don't understand anything, kid," Pots said.

"This is the way it's always been. You can't change it."

With that he walked past me, moving down the line like a sergeant inspecting his troops. When he got to Warren, he raised his arm high in the air and struck him with the back of his hand. Warren dropped like a stone, tried to get to his knees, then fell flat on his back in the dirt.

"Help him," he ordered the other two.

But Catface had already collapsed and Arthur was down on one knee trying to get him back to standing.

Pots turned to me and held his arm out to show me what he could still do.

"Nothing's changed, in this place or any other place," he said. "That's where they belong. And they know it."

He put his arm across my shoulder like we'd been friends forever and moved me to the far sidewalk, where he'd left his half-sized bat leaning against the wall. He pushed me down to the sidewalk, then picked up the weapon and sat beside me.

"All I have to do is pull the trigger," he said, pretending the bat was a Lee-Enfield rifle.

"You tried to knock us off the wagonload of shiplap. You wanted to kill us with that bat."

He put his hand on my knee and squeezed.

"I know where you've been, and I know what you know."

"What are you going to do?"

"Nothing," he said, looking at Warren. "I don't have to. He'll be dead before long."

I turned to Warren and saw what Pots saw. Old Joe's eyes blinked slowly, as if there was hardly any strength in him to do more. His hand had gone limp and the bottle of whiskey lay in the street.

"I can do something," I said, and grabbed for his bat. He moved it no more than an inch but I missed it. He slapped me across the face. I tried to turn away, but he slapped me again.

"You can't stop me," Pots said.

I sat in the gravel and rubbed the stinging from my cheek.

"You're not part of this." Pots pointed to Warren. "Only he is."

"Help me up," Warren whispered.

Pots moved his open hand toward Warren like I was welcome to go and do what I could. Arthur had got Joe to one knee. In another second, we had him standing.

"Take a drink," I whispered, and clamped his hard hand around the bottle.

"I don't need it now," he said, and pushed us away. "I don't need nothing."

Pots stood as still as death.

Warren moved slowly across the street, his head and shoulders to one side like he was drunk. He swung the whiskey bottle at Pots's face, but missed without Pots having to move a muscle and fell at Pots's feet. Pots set his cowboy boot on Warren's bare chest and shrugged.

As Pots set his foot back on the ground, I charged him.

He knocked me backward into the street.

Arthur charged, and next thing we lay together looking up. As my head fell away from the moment, I saw Grandpa move between the buildings lining the south side of Main Street, the sacred pipe in his hand.

"You weren't there," Pots said to Grandpa. "You have no power here."

Grandpa kneeled at Warren's side.

I was sitting now, helping Arthur up.

Next to Warren's hand was the whiskey bottle, as empty as last night, when Grandpa had poured the liquid into the fire.

Grandpa began singing his Blackfoot song, holding the pipe to the sky, moving it toward the four corners of the earth, the song growing as his words reached out to the great dome of God's sweat lodge. He smoked the sacred pipe, then passed it to Warren, lying in the dirt. Warren smoked, too. I felt my throat burn like I had taken a turn. As Catface moved to Warren's side, Grandpa lifted his hand like he had when he tossed the sacred plants onto the glowing river stones.

"I was there," Grandpa said. "I am part of this." He flung dark powder into Pots's face. It flashed red, as bright as the sun, in the white August light.

The Mark of a Coward

Pots cupped his hands over his eyes as he stumbled backward, his heels hooking the sidewalk lip, knocking him flat. He screamed as he thrashed from side to side on the concrete, then he became horribly still.

When he finally got to his feet, cussing and spitting, Warren was standing, facing him.

Pots's eyes looked like he'd taken a blast of chlorine gas.

"Finally found a friend with some balls, did ya?" Pots said. "Dirty, rotten, cheating son of a —"

Pots never finished the cuss. Warren moved quickly forward like a young soldier attacking an enemy trench. He swung his arm in a wide overhand arch and struck Pots on the side of the head with the flat of the whiskey bottle. Shards of glass exploded past Pots's head, clung to his hair and fell at his feet. Blood oozed from the wound under his white hair. For a few seconds, Pots just stood there with his arms hanging limp. His eyes rolled back, he swayed in a slow circle, then fell backward, landing on his back on the sidewalk again.

Warren dropped with a knee across Pots's chest and pushed Pots's face to one side until his cheek was flat on the hot concrete, exposing his neck to the jagged remains of the whiskey bottle.

"No!" I called.

Catface wrapped his thin arms around my neck and dropped me face-first into the gravel.

A car skidded to a stop.

A door slammed and feet ran quickly toward us.

Over the bits of gravel and arms and the top of Warren's bare back, I saw the bottle slice down at Pots. His feet went stiff then shook in the deadly still August air.

I tried to close my eyes, but something was forcing me to look, to be a witness to this event.

Grandpa was standing with his hand held out. Warren placed the broken whiskey bottle in Grandpa's palm and they both stared down at Pots lying in a pool of blood.

Grandpa spoke some low Blackfoot words into Warren's ear.

Warren nodded slowly and backed out into the street, clutching his hand over his heart, his chin turned slightly upward, and his eyes looking up at God's great dome. In the next second, he was lying in the gravel.

I was the first to reach him. When I lifted my fist to strike his chest like Arthur had done, he raised his hand and stopped me. Instead, I set my hand on his chest and felt the slow beat of his heart. His lips moved as if he was trying to speak.

I put my ear close and listened to his last few breaths. It seemed he spoke in the old Blackfoot Grandpa used, words that were familiar to me: "He talks for Indians?"

"What?" I whispered. "I don't understand what you mean."

I waited with my hand still over his chest. As the beat of his heart faded into memory, the deep lines softened on his face and his mouth turned upward, as if he had learned to smile again.

Grandpa began a song in Blackfoot that made my heart come up into my throat and the tears roll down my cheeks.

Jane and Emma Howe stood at the front bumper of Jane's big black Dodge, looking as if they might never move again.

From the corner of my eye, I could see Pots's feet begin to move. He got to his knees, then sat back on the sidewalk. He pressed his hand to his head and made a moaning sound. With a single heave he was standing. He pulled his shirttail out and tore the buttons loose, popping them into the street. The bullet wounds I had seen on his chest were now stained red with his blood, as if Vimy Ridge was living on the streets of Grayson. He wrapped the shirt around his hand and pressed it to his cheek, then pulled it away and stared at the blood pattern.

Across his face, above the line where his whiskers grew, was a deep wound, cut into his face with glass.

The shape of a feather, now the pink of newly opened flesh that would soon scar to white, where no amount of sun could make anything more of it than what it was.

The mark of a coward.

He turned away up the alley.

Emma, still too sore to move without her sister's help, had knelt by my side and touched Warren's face like a mother would touch her child. Under my hand, I felt his chest fall, as if he had waited for her touch before he could release his last breath.

Jane set her arm across my shoulders and put her face softly on my hair, like maybe that would help her stop crying. Within her jerky breaths, I thought I heard her say, "Do you know who translated Treaty Number 7 for the Indian people?"

When I turned to her, she was already looking at me.

"A white man talked for the Indians," I said.

I could feel the heat rise in my face as her cheeks reddened and a faint smile pushed aside the tears.

"Jerry Potts," I said, "he talked for the Indians."

She looked down at Warren's soft face. In that instant, I knew the letter was from Warren and the words he had written, "He talks for Indians," had nothing to do with Jerry Potts. They had to do with Roy Potter, with Pots. Joe Warren had told anybody who read the letter that Pots had killed Wilfred Black.

My Friend. He Is Dead.

There were as many Indian people at Joe Warren's funeral as there were whites, and there were quite a few of those. Of course Pots wasn't there, even though he'd always claimed he was Old Joe's only true friend.

Somebody said Pots had snuck out of town late one night; somebody else said he'd hanged himself in his own basement. I believed he'd be back in his insurance office pretending nothing had happened, but we'd all see the scar and know he was not just a liar, but a coward. In time, everybody would know who he really was.

The whole Samson family sat together in the back pew because Mom couldn't get us all ready at the same time, so we were late, and all the front seats were filled up with people who weren't.

Arthur's grandpa sat right up front, his long gray hair in braids over his buckskin-covered shoulders. Beside him sat Arthur and his family. Across the aisle sat Emma, Catface, and Jane. All of us in our family groups.

I sat staring at the reverend wondering what he'd

have to say to all these different people that would give them the comfort they came for. I knew Warren had died happy, and I'd bet a year's worth of gopher tail bounty that he was still smiling inside his coffin.

The reverend looked slowly over the Indian faces, then back over the white faces.

"Joe Warren was a sinner, suffering mightily at his own hand. Yet he has been redeemed from the deepest pit. By whom?" The reverend looked across the rows of bowed heads, the slightest hint of a grin on his face. "Not some pagan god masked with superstition. It was the Holy Redeemer. The One Savior. The Son of the true God. Our Lord Jesus Christ. Let it been known that He has done His work here for all of us to see, and He has picked the worst among you to show the rest of us the way."

Arthur looked back at me and rolled his eyes. Mom touched my arm, her hanky already wet with her tears. When she pulled me close and kissed the top of my head, I thought I saw the shape of a bull buffalo in a dream moving above us all on the heat rising from the people. From somewhere came the old Blackfoot word *Apistotoki*, Creator. I knew then there was really just one God, and that He takes many forms.

I had my head down and was praying for every soul on Vimy Ridge when I felt a hand on my shoulder pushing me gently along the pew toward Mom. A man sat, placed his black cowboy hat on his long legs and bowed his head, his shoulder-length black hair hanging over his face.

I thought I heard him whispering, "*Napi akaiiniu.*" My friend. He is dead.

When the service ending, our eyes were all red and swollen, and our hankies were so wet we couldn't put them in our pockets. We filed slowly past the reverend, all quietly shaking his hand for the good job he had done sending Joe Warren's soul on its eternal trip.

I stood at the bottom of the steps and watched as the reverend shook the hand of the man who wore the black cowboy hat.

"Thank you for coming," the reverend said. "Do I know you?"

"My name is Apisi-Moykatsis."

"Did you know Joe Warren well?"

"Yes," he said, "but that was a long time ago."

"May the Lord be with you during your time of grief."

The man nodded. As he walked past me, he pulled his cowboy hat down low, nearly covering his eyes. He was very young.

I gave Mom a kiss on the cheek and stuffed my bow tie into her dress pocket. She pinched my cheek, then softly patted the red spot she'd made with her touch.

I walked down Main Street with the cars and trucks and horses and wagons all working their way slowly to the graveyard. I guess I wandered around more than I walked anyplace in particular. I kept wondering why people prayed. I wondered if it was really to get the thing they prayed for or just to talk themselves into living without it.

I prayed for Joe Warren to go to a good place. I prayed God would see some good in his heart. I prayed Warren and Wilfred Black would meet on the other side and go fishing, that they would be friends forever.

When I got done wondering and wishing and praying, I was standing in the alley at the foot of the wooden stairs leading up to Warren's room.

A dark shadow moved across the thin curtain hanging in the window.

All the Way to Forever

I took a big breath and slowly let it out. I didn't want there to be things left to do at the end of Warren's last day above ground.

I rolled my sleeves, and headed up the stairs. I knocked harder on the door than I'd intended to and almost yelled when I spoke.

"Joe Warren's dead," I said. "Can't you leave him be? Can't you show some respect?"

When no one answered, I eased the door open.

A black cowboy hat sat in the middle of the wooden table. The tall Indian man was sitting in Warren's chair, his head forward, as he moved a small pile of old photographs between his hands.

I stood at his side and pushed easy on his shoulder. When he slid to the far side of the chair, I sat down, took the photograph of Joe Warren and Wilfred Black from my shirt pocket and placed it between his hands.

He stared at it for a very long time.

I took Old Man Howe's forty dollars from my back pocket and set it on the photograph.

"Old Man Howe gave me this to test me," I said.

"He said it was to run the Indian off his land. If I didn't, I'd be a dishonest man, a liar, a cheat, no better than he was."

"He has a way with money," the man said, and placed his hand over the bills. "Forty dollars will take me a long distance."

I held the door while he slipped the photo and the money into his pocket, pulled his cowboy hat down, nearly covering his eyes, and walked down the wooden steps to the gravel alley.

"Apisi-Moykatsis," I finally said, "Wolfleg."

"As I remember it," he said, and walked down the alley, heading toward the highway, all the way to forever.